Praise for

Record Scratch

"J.J. Hensley's tale of a stoic PI investigating the murder of a has-been rock star is equal parts classic whodunnit and gritty noir, peppered with high-octane action scenes that will leave you breathless. *Record Scratch* is like a throat punch: powerful, shocking, and unapologetic, but the surprising poignant ending will stay with you a long after you've finished the book. This is a thriller that crackles from the first page to the last."

—Jennifer Hillier,
author of *Jar of Hearts*

"*Record Scratch* shocks you out of your ordinary groove. Sometimes witty, other times haunting, but when the needle jumps the track, the body count screams."

—Marc E. Fitch,
author of *Paradise Burns* and *Dirty Water*

"In *Record Scratch*, Hensley gifts us with a bounty of goods: a solid mystery, a damaged but relatable main character—one you root for, and swift plotting that weaves a compelling, compulsive tale of music and death and the demons carried by those in law enforcement. Bring me more Trevor!"

—Shannon Kirk, international bestselling
author of *Method 15/33*

"...a tersely written and tightly plotted gem, featuring one of the most unique protagonists around, Trevor Galloway. The book is action-packed with a dash of mordant wit, and I can't wait to read more in this intense, engaging series."

—David Bell, *USA Today* bestselling
author of *Somebody's Daughter*

Praise for
the works of J.J. Hensley

"Crime writer J.J. Hensley deserves readers' attention and trust, because beyond his ever-stronger prose, he brings his ex-badge carrier's street smart eyes to this hard world we live in. Put him on your READ list."

—James Grady, author of
Six Days of the Condor

"Fast-paced and funny, *Bolt Action Remedy* is an action-packed thriller that will keep readers guessing until the final page."

—Rebecca Drake, author of *Only Ever You*

"*Bolt Action Remedy* is entertaining as hell."

—Andrew Pyper, award-winning
author of *The Damned*

"It's about time somebody gave Hannibal Lecter a run for his money. J.J. Hensley's *Measure Twice* is up to the task."

—Gwen Florio, award-winning
author of *Montana and Dakota*

"This artfully constructed mystery makes effective use of the third-rate-college setting and of Pittsburgh"

—*Publishers Weekly*

"J.J. Hensley's debut novel is a lean, fast-paced, suspenseful murder mystery—told with style, intelligence, and wit."

—John Verdon, bestselling
Author of *Let the Devil Sleep*

RECORD
SCRATCH

OTHER BOOKS BY J.J. HENSLEY

Trevor Galloway Thrillers
Bolt Action Remedy

Resolve
Measure Twice
Chalk's Outline

J.J. HENSLEY

RECORD
SCRATCH

A TREVOR GALLOWAY THRILLER

Down and Out Books
3959 Van Dyke Road, Suite 265
Lutz, FL 33558
www.DownAndOutBooks.com

Cover design by JT Lindroos

ISBN: 1-948235-35-8
ISBN-13: 978-1-948235-35-8

To Kasia and Cassie
My heart and soul

Life is for the living, death is for the dead.
Let life be like music, and death a note unsaid.
—Langston Hughes

UNTITLED JIMMY SPARTAN ALBUM

Track 1: You Puzzle Me
Track 2: Listen and Learn
Track 3: Picture Imperfect
Track 4: Always a Woman
Track 5: Complicated
Track 6: Broken Compass
Track 7: Like a Hole in the Head
Track 8: Fooled Me Twice (The Heart of Shame)
Track 9: A Sheep in Wolf's Clothing
Track 10: An Early Wake-up Fall
Track 11: One Last Shove
Track 12: Fight to the Breath

PROLOGUE

There are two types of men you must fear in this world: Men who have everything to lose and men who have nothing to lose. Their common thread is desperation and—if backed into a corner—either man will turn that thread into a wire and wrap it around your throat. Of course, there are different levels of desperation. I suppose it all goes back to Maslow's hierarchy of needs. If visualized as a pyramid, the bottom three layers consist of a human being's most fundamental needs: physiological requirements, safety, and a sense of love and belonging. If one satisfies these, then an individual may strive to obtain the needs found on the top two layers, esteem and self-actualization. It's a nice, neat hierarchy and I tend to believe the theory is fairly accurate.

I've seen what happens when one person assaults another's pyramid. In a general sense, if you jeopardize self-esteem or limit the ability to realize full potential, usually the worst you will get is a harshly spoken word followed by a cold shoulder. However, if you threaten another's sense of being loved, or put their physical well-being at risk, then you could find yourself being murdered—which, not coincidentally, is my present situation.

I can't see my aggressor and cannot be sure of his identity, but I feel I'm on the brink of a revelation. He's powerful and has the advantage. My back arches as he pulls hard, nearly lifting me off my feet, my toes helplessly tapping on the floor. I feel a trickle of blood roll down my neck as something relentlessly constricts, and my peripheral vision blurs before it finally vanishes. The funny thing about losing my ability to see objects at the edge of my vision is that now I've been forced to focus on what is right in front of me. As the narrow tunnel of vision closes completely, I find I have nowhere to look but deep inside of myself. The foundations of my pyramid are crumbling, but my mind is clear. Something primal awakens and now I know exactly where I stand.

There are two types of men you must fear in this world: Men who have everything to lose—and men like me.

TRACK 1
"YOU PUZZLE ME"

Eight days prior

"You won't sign?"

"I won't," I replied.

"It's a fairly standard non-disclosure agreement."

"It's not *my* standard," I said, sliding the paper back across the desk.

"Mr. Galloway, you have to appreciate my position. I wish to hire you because of your reputation for discretion."

"Why is your hair pink?" I asked.

She paused. "I change it every month. This month is pink. Last month it was blue. I like a little variety now and then."

"What color will it be next month?" I asked.

She shrugged.

I nodded and swiveled my chair, taking in my surroundings. Tracy Bermindo's office walls were covered with concert photos, album covers, and framed ticket stubs. If I wouldn't have known I'd just driven across the Warhol Bridge, I'd think I was in L.A., not Pittsburgh. The downtown high-rise provided views of the city's North Shore, including the baseball and football stadiums. I shuddered to think what kind of price tag was attached to the twenty-third floor office. Regardless, Tracy Bermindo's talent management business was doing well.

"Why do you ask about my hair?"

"Curious," I replied. "I wondered if you were a singer like your brother."

Her expression changed and I could see I'd offended her. I wasn't surprised. My stoic demeanor and habit of asking direct questions does that from time to time.

"My brother was not *just* a singer, Mr. Galloway."

"Please, call me Trevor."

She sat forward and placed her arms on the desk. I noticed her pupils were large and her eyes were bloodshot.

"Trevor, not only could Jimmy sing, but he could play seven different instruments and was a brilliant songwriter," she said rapidly. "He was one of the last true musicians, not one of these prime-time pop stars collecting votes on a television show. Jimmy was inspired by the best and he inspired others to be better."

She leaned back a few inches and took a series of quick breaths. I couldn't be sure, but she seemed in the habit of having to calm herself down. Tracy closed her eyes and when she opened them again her expression was calm, but firm. She looked me square in the eye—well, both eyes—and concluded, "He was not, as you said, a *singer.*"

A normal person would manage to turn the corners of their mouth in an upward direction to express a sincere, conciliatory grin before apologizing. Not being good at smiling, I went straight for the apology.

"I meant no disrespect, Mrs. Bermindo. I'm somewhat ignorant when it comes to the terms you use in the industry."

Even absent a smile, I must have conveyed some amount of earnestness because she leaned all the way back in her leather chair and the redness that had accumulated in her face appeared to dissipate. With the pink hair, gold jacket, and flushed face, she was a rainbow of emotions and my instincts were telling me my potential client might be unpredictable.

"Sorry," she said. "I'm still struggling with my brother's death and I get very defensive of his reputation. As an agent and publicist, I'm used to dealing with industry types and I sometimes forget that not everyone speaks the language."

I nodded.

"And it is miss, by the way," she informed me. "I'm not married."

I didn't speak, not wanting to make another misstep and end up stumbling into a conversation about a previous divorce, or whatever reason she had for using a different last name than her brother. Seeing she was experiencing a series of emotions, I decided to tread lightly, but I wasn't going to relent and sign the non-disclosure agreement. The problem was I needed the job. But, I've found the best way to land a job is to act like you don't *need* the job. As an unlicensed private investigator, I can pull off the part, since I obviously don't need the work enough to go get officially licensed. At least that's what I tell myself.

She glanced at a photo on a bookshelf. It was different than the ones on the walls. It wasn't of Jimmy Spartan playing at a club or smiling and laughing with members of his band. In the small silver frame, was a faded photo of a young Jimmy Spartan and his younger sister Tracy, standing on a sidewalk in Pittsburgh's Strip District. From their clothes, I surmised the photo was taken sometime in the eighties when Jimmy was maybe all of fifteen years old and his sibling had barely broken double-digits.

Without taking her eyes off the photo, she said, "Marriages come and go in the music business, Trevor. But, siblings have a special bond. When my brother took the stage name Jimmy Spartan, I actually thought about changing mine too. I was so proud of him and I wanted everyone to know Jimmy was my brother."

The lady who was still in mourning let out an odd giggle, but when she turned back toward me her eyes were damp. "Our dad was no good, but my mom was decent enough. I kept the Bermindo name to honor her. She died not long after that photo was taken. We moved in with our uncle, but Jimmy was the one who looked out for me while we were growing up. He never turned his back on me, even when he hit the big time. It's the way he was. Loyalty. It's the reason that while he had a residence in L.A., he kept his primary home here in Pittsburgh. It's the reason he let me be his representative when he could have gone with any agency in the country. Because of him, I was able to build a successful business and maintain offices here, in L.A., and in New York."

She grabbed a tissue from a box on the desk and dabbed her eyes.

After clearing her throat as gently as I've ever heard anyone do so, she smiled and said, "Loyalty is the reason I called you."

I waited.

She sat up and the smile vanished as if it had never been conceived. Whatever emotional trip this lady was taking, the vehicle she was using was a high-speed roller coaster.

"In addition to representing musicians, my agency handles public relations for several corporations. One of those companies is Mountain Resource Solutions."

I blinked.

"I was told you did some work for them a while back and I was assured you are a man who can be trusted with matters of a delicate nature."

Now it was my turn to sit up straight.

I said, "Without permission, I can't discuss any work I've

done for any of my previous clients." I liked the way that sounded. It came across as official and business-like. The fact I had only ever had one client and that client was in fact the CEO of Mountain Resources Solutions was irrelevant.

Tracy smiled, "That's exactly why I want to hire you, Trevor. I need someone I can trust to keep private matters private. My brother's reputation is everything at this point. I want justice, but I want it administered...quietly."

I didn't like the sound of that one bit. For a moment, I thought she had misunderstood what skill set I could bring to the table.

"Miss Bermindo—"

"Call me Tracy."

"Tracy...I need to be clear about something. I'm not a hitter. I keep things to myself, but I don't kill people."

That was true. But not completely. I'd killed before, out of necessity.

She seemed taken aback, and then having replayed her own words in her head, she laughed a genuine laugh that was akin to a cackle.

"Oh, no, no, no," she said while the reducing her volume to a chuckle. "I'm sorry. I don't want you to hurt anybody. I simply need you to look into my brother's murder and develop amnesia if...convenient to his memory."

Part of me wondered if I should be embarrassed for mis-interpreting her words, but another part of me wondered if I had in fact read the subtext accurately.

"Tracy," I said. "Your brother was murdered nearly eight months ago and the police investigated the case thoroughly. I'm not sure what you think I can do."

"How do you know?" she asked.

I tilted my head. "How do I know...what?"

"How do you know they investigated the case thoroughly?"

I took a breath and remembered the nonstop newspaper

coverage, the local politicians posing for the cameras, and the tributes to a hometown musician who left the world too soon.

"As I'm sure you know, I was a narcotics detective. I get how much pressure is on the PD when the victim of a crime is high-profile like your brother. I assure you the department left no stone unturned."

Her face darkened. "They missed something."

"What makes you say that?"

"Because nobody's been arrested for Jimmy's murder."

Silence filled the room for several seconds.

"I want you to sign the agreement," she said, sliding the paper my way.

"I can't."

"Why?"

I inhaled deeply and then spoke. "I have no intention of running to a tabloid and selling a story, or talking to any reporters for that matter. However, if I somehow uncover evidence that could directly identify Jimmy's murderer, then I have to take it to the police."

"I understand," she said. "But what about facts not directly related to the identification of the killer?"

I stared at her and she at me.

"What is it you want to keep quiet, Tracy?"

She swallowed hard and seemed to debate how far she was willing to trust a stranger. If she'd done any real digging, then she had to know my professional history was sketchy at best.

Finally, she explained, "Jimmy was taking drugs."

I held my hands out in a gesture that should have been interpreted as, 'Duh.'

"Tracy," I said in a tone I hoped was patient. "Jimmy was a rock star who cut his teeth in the eighties. He sang songs professing his love for drugs. His biggest album was titled *Two Line Rush*. His naked body was found covered in cocaine."

I paused to give her a chance to respond.

When she didn't speak, I finally said, "I think the cat may be out of the bag about his drug use."

She shook her head. "Not those kind of drugs." She started to say something else, but stopped herself.

"I really am going to have to insist on the non-disclosure agreement," she said. "I'll pay well above your standard fee."

I tried to recall my standard fee, but then I remembered I didn't have one. I'd been paid very well for the case involving Mountain Resources Solutions and had been living off those funds, along with my disability retirement pension, ever since. The pension helped, but the proceeds were dwindling fast. I understood Tracy's concern for her brother's reputation, such as it was, but I held my ground and pushed the paper back across the desk.

"Unless something I uncover can lead to someone else being seriously harmed, my lips are sealed."

She pondered, "I assume if you break confidentiality then you could lose your license."

"I don't have a license," I admitted.

"Why not?"

"So nobody can take it away from me."

She reached into a desk drawer and pulled out a manila envelope.

Tracy tossed it across the desk and said, "Here is ten thousand dollars in cash. I don't want a receipt or any record of this transaction. I've made arrangements that if you solve the case and preserve my brother's reputation, you will receive another ten thousand."

I stared at the envelope before saying, "What drugs?"

She tapped an index finger on the oak in front of her. She did so deliberately and for such a long time, that I thought she might break a nail.

"He was on Donepezel," she finally said.

I'd worked narcotics for a long time, but that didn't sound familiar.

"It's a treatment for memory loss, associated with early Alzheimer's disease," she said.

"I don't remember reading about it in the papers," I said. "If it was discovered during the autopsy, then it appears the medical examiner and investigating detectives kept it quiet."

Tracy said, "I know. As next of kin, the detectives filled me in on the results and never mentioned any medications. I didn't specifically ask about the drug, because I didn't want to give the story birth if the meds had gone undetected. We were at the point that I had to handle many of Jimmy's day-to-day affairs, even beyond my role as his agent. Jimmy was having a real tough time. The disease was taking everything away from him—piece by piece."

Tracy rubbed her eyes and now the tears started to fall in earnest.

I shrugged and said, "It happens." The words had slipped out as the thought had formed in my mind. As is my habit, I unintentionally came across cold.

Tracy furrowed her brow and said sharply, "I'd heard your nickname, and now I see how it was acquired."

She stood and pointed to the door.

I held up a hand. "I apologize. I didn't mean it that way. What I meant was, it's not unheard of for a person his age to be diagnosed with the disease. I'm just wondering why you think it would damage his reputation. If anything, people would *sympathize* with Jimmy. He might end up being a rallying call for early Alzheimer's awareness. It could be a good thing."

Tracy unclenched her jaw and sat back down.

"You don't understand," she said. "Jimmy finished recording a new album last winter. He'd been battling the disease for the past two years and it took a toll on his music.

He sent me a digital copy of the album and…it wasn't good."

"How not good?" I asked.

"I hadn't told Jimmy, but the record label wasn't going to release it unless it was shortened and totally reworked."

I didn't know much about the music business, but I knew if a label was refusing to release an album by an artist as well-known as Jimmy Spartan, the product had to have been bad or completely contrary to the label's expectations.

"I think I'm starting to get the picture," I said. "You want me to look into Jimmy's murder, and you want me to make sure the topic of Alzheimer's never comes up."

She nodded. "As of now, nobody seems to know about the diagnosis. When the label called to tell me they weren't happy with the record, I made up an excuse about Jimmy being in and out of rehab and how he just needed to get straight, like he always had in the past. They bought the story."

"I still don't understand," I said. "It seems the damage to Jimmy's reputation would be minimal. People get sick. Terrible things happen. Your brother had a great run and will be remembered as a great musician."

"You're right," she said. "But, Jimmy's last record could harm his legacy. He shouldn't be remembered for that album."

I thought about that for a moment and then said, "I'm not sure your concerns are warranted. Other than you, only the record label received a copy. You both have a vested interest in not letting it see the light of day, so those copies should be safe. Who else has a copy?"

"Only one person," she said. "Jimmy's killer."

I waited.

"Jimmy loved vinyl records," she said. "Each time he recorded a new album, the minute he finished he had one special vinyl album made to commemorate the event. He kept it in his house."

"And it's missing?" I asked.

"Jimmy was killed in his house, I wasn't allowed to go through his things for several days. However, I've searched every square inch of the place since and I can't find it anywhere. He had shown it to me two days before the murder and I'm sure he wouldn't have let it out of his sight. I think whoever killed Jimmy took the record."

"Why?" I asked.

She tossed her hands up and became animated. "I have no idea. To ruin Jimmy? As a keepsake? Who knows? But, I do know it's been eight months and the police are no closer to finding the person who did this. How did someone break into Jimmy's house, manage to smash his head in with a microphone stand, and *not* leave behind any incriminating evidence? How? You tell me. How?"

I waited for the latest wave to subside and allowed her to collect herself.

"You really don't show much emotion, do you?" she asked. "Is that why people started calling you the Tin Man? No heart?"

I didn't say anything.

She rubbed a hand through her hair, leaving one side in disarray. "So, will you take the case?"

I nodded. "I'll do my best."

"Do I have your word that you will pursue every lead and do your best to protect Jimmy's name?"

"You do."

She reached in the same drawer from which she'd retrieved the envelope of cash, and pulled out a card that had a name and number printed across the front.

"Upon completion of the job, please contact my assistant Melody for the remainder of your payment."

"I will," I said. "I'll contact you periodically to give you updates."

Her hand disappeared again into the drawer. I assumed she was going to hand me a card that contained her personal phone number. While she did this, I stood, picked up the envelope of cash, and looked down as I slid it inside my jacket. I raised my eyes while extending my hand to take the next card she was going to hand me.

"We won't be speaking with each other again," she said, putting a loaded revolver under her chin. She pulled the trigger.

TRACK 2
"LISTEN AND LEARN"

I shifted uncomfortably on the couch with which I was all too familiar. A window was open and an autumn breeze carried the faint scent of burning leaves. My mind drifted back to early childhood memories of October school days in my hometown of Atlanta. In Georgia, the summer heat clung to the streets well into October or early November. Here, the tenth month on the calendar represented the few precious weeks when the grip of humidity loosened on a city that would soon battle a tough winter.

"Do you feel responsible for the woman's death?" she asked.

I shifted again.

"I'm not sure," I replied. "I could see she was unstable, but I didn't realize..."

She tapped a pen against a legal pad and crossed her long legs in a motion so smooth her chair failed to swivel an inch.

Sliding designer eyeglasses up the bridge of her nose, she said, "Earlier, you told me the police had discovered this person..." she paused and looked at me expectantly.

"Tracy," I said.

"Yes. Tracy. You mentioned the police learned of a previous suicide attempt."

I gave a nod, rubbed a hand over my face, and noticed the stubble. I'd forgotten to shave. It had been three days since Tracy Bermindo had used a .38 Smith & Wesson to take her own life. Only three days. Had I shaved since?

"Do you believe there is anything you could have done to stop her?"

"Perhaps," I said. "But I was viewing her as a future client, not a risk."

Dr. Lana Welch jotted something on her notepad. I've always wondered what psychiatrists' notes looked like. Are they insightful bits of shorthand, or meaningless scribbles meant to give off the appearance of thoughtful analysis?

"But that isn't your training, is it?" she asked in a way that made it clear it wasn't a question. "As a police officer, you were trained to identify people who might pose a threat to you or someone else. It appears Tracy posed a threat to no one but herself."

I shook my head. "No. I've had training and experience in dealing with emotionally disturbed individuals. All of the signs were there, but I was more concerned about securing a paying job."

I thought about the flashes of rage, sadness, and even the inappropriate laughter Tracy had displayed in her office that day. The behavioral cues paired with some physical indications of drug abuse, such as the dilated pupils, should have set off some of my internal alarms. But, I wanted to get paid.

"Let me ask you this: How long was your conversation with Tracy?"

I recalled the time I arrived at Tracy's office and tried to remember what time it was when I pulled out my cell phone and called nine-one-one. After dealing with the initial shock, I'd started to use Tracy's desk phone to call the police, but it had been covered with blood. I'd waited for the

cops to arrive and spent the next two hours being interviewed by the responding patrol officer and then a detective from the Violent Crime Unit. Since, I'd left the department several years prior, I didn't know either man. Unfortunately, the detective, a lanky guy named F.J. Case, recognized my name and knew my reputation. Even after my
hands had tested negative for gunshot residue, he still radi-
ated a subtle animosity in my direction.

"Trevor?"

"What? I'm sorry. I think Tracy and I spoke for about
twenty minutes."

"And do you think her descent toward suicide started
when you walked through her doorway?"

"Of course not," I said.

"Then isn't it likely you happened to be a bystander at a
tragic moment that was the result of a chain of events that
began long ago?"

I stared across the room and through the open window.

"Are you thinking about using?" she asked.

"You know the answer to that," I said abruptly.

"In the past, you've been tempted to—"

"No," I repeated, cutting her off mid-sentence. I didn't
raise my voice. I rarely do. But, the tone of my response
was on the hard side of direct.

The room emptied of all sounds other than a pen making dark indentations on a yellow sheet of paper.

After half a minute, she said, "I do have to admit, I'm
surprised you're seeing me today. It's been a while since
we've spoken."

"I suppose."

With a smile, she said, "And now, here we are."

On the occasions she smiled, I was reminded of how
beautiful she was. If not for our complicated relationship,
she'd probably be my type.

As if reading my mind, she said, "Last we spoke, you had ended your relationship with the physician you were seeing. I believe her name is Raylene? Have you reconsidered that decision?"

I sighed, which she correctly interpreted to mean that my status as a single man in his forties was intact.

"Are you still comfortable with your reasons for breaking things off?"

"You mean the fact I'm a former junkie who has been targeted by members of a violent drug network and I have a history of hallucinations?" I asked rhetorically and without emotion.

Dr. Welch uncrossed her legs and used one of her hands to straighten out her navy blue skirt.

She said, "I think it's time we talk about these reasons you have."

"What is there to discuss?" I asked, looking around in every direction but hers. "Facts are facts."

"Except when they aren't."

"Well, that's deep," I said sarcastically. "Remind me, how much am I paying you for this session?"

She smiled again. Damn, she had a great smile. If I weren't immune to the ailment of emotional displays, I'd have said it was contagious.

Putting the notepad aside, she said, "You did not become addicted to heroin by choice. Don't you believe being forcibly injected with narcotics by drug dealers who were holding you captive is cause to give yourself a break?"

I swallowed hard. "I gave up operational details. I gave up names. Informants—one of which ended up dead."

"You were tortured and drugged," said Dr. Welch. "Nobody can fault you for what you said under those circumstances."

"Sure they can," I countered. "Plenty of cops do, at least

subconsciously. I can feel it, you know. I felt it with the detective who talked to me the other day. Once he realized who I was, it was clear he would have loved nothing more than to put cuffs on my wrists."

"Even if it *is* true that some individuals resent you, do you think it's reasonable for them feel that way?"

"Yes," I said truthfully.

She seemed ready to argue the point, but chose to move on.

"One of your other reasons for keeping people at a distance is that you believe you are being targeted by members of the same drug gang that kept you prisoner."

"Of course," I said in a matter of fact tone.

"Because you harmed their organization," she said.

"I killed one of the men who abducted me and played a role in the organization's top enforcer being locked away. So, yes. I harmed them."

"All of that happened quite a while ago. Have there been any indications that the group is coming after you?"

I didn't answer.

"Trevor, I'd like you to respond."

Finally, I said, "I can't be certain."

"Why aren't you certain?" she asked.

I looked at her and said, "You know why."

She removed her glasses and placed them in her lap.

"Because of the hallucinations," she said.

Although we'd addressed the subject before, I leaned forward to explain. "When I'm on my meds, my senses are dulled and I can't think straight. Ten guys could be following me and I'd never know. With those pills, it takes every ounce of my concentration to hold up my end of a conversation. When I don't take my meds, I'm sharp and notice things few others do. But, when I'm not taking them..."

She picked up her notepad and started writing again.

As the pen danced, she said, "When you're off your medication, you can't be sure who or what is real."

I stood, walked to the open window, and surveyed the cloudless afternoon. The wind hit my face and I closed my eyes. In spite of recent events, I felt good. The layer of fog in my mind had been lifting for a while. Three days, in fact.

From behind me, Dr. Welch said, "You're going to work the Jimmy Spartan case, aren't you?"

"I don't know."

"Yes, you do."

In the distance, a train whistle sounded.

Without turning to look at Dr. Welch, I asked, "What makes you say that?"

She allowed herself a small laugh and said, "Because why else would you be here talking to me?"

The next morning, Chase Vinson met me at the gate of Jimmy Spartan's property in the North Hills. Between thick wrought iron bars, I could see a black driveway snaking its way up to an enormous house, partially hidden by mature bur oaks. Chase was the only friend I had left in the department, and while the Spartan homicide wasn't his case, his solid reputation as an investigator in the Robbery Squad meant he could ask for favors. Favors like being granted access into the Spartan house.

He pulled his massive frame out of his unmarked Ford, and walked over to me. "I lied for you."

We shook hands. "What did you tell the lead detective?"

"That I had an informant at a pawn shop claiming that someone was going around bragging about having lifted some memorabilia from the Spartan house."

"They bought that?" I asked.

Fighting off the morning chill, he blew into his hands

before retrieving a slip of paper from his pocket. "I told them it was a bullshit tip, but that I needed to cover my ass."

After taking three large strides toward a keypad mounted into a stone pillar, he pressed a series of buttons while reading off the yellow Post-It note. From behind the pillar, a motor hummed and the gate began moving off to the side.

"Let's leave our cars out here and walk up," Chase suggested while gesturing toward the house. "After you."

We walked up the driveway a while in silence before I said, "Thanks. For lying, I mean."

He waved it away, but I knew better.

"You could have told them the truth." It was a dumb statement to make. If word got out that Chase was helping out a former cop who had fallen from grace, and then fell even further, every move he made in the future would be scrutinized. Of course, Chase wouldn't acknowledge this truth. He never did.

"Screw 'em," he spouted off. "It's none of their business." Changing the subject, he scanned the grounds. "This is quite a place."

It was. The lawn was manicured, the hedges trimmed, and the mulch around the landscaping fresh. The previous evening, I'd called Chase to enlist his help and he'd immediately done some checking around. He'd discovered that nobody had moved into the house after Jimmy's death and all of the furnishings were still in place. The property looked absolutely amazing for a site that had been unoccupied for the better part of a year.

Before I could ask, Chase said, "The lead detective is Jacobs. He told me the grounds keeping service is under contract for another two months. There was a housekeeping service as well, but they stopped showing up after the murder. Jimmy left the house to his sister, but she never moved in and kind of kept it as a shrine to her brother."

Chase stopped walking, turned my direction and grabbed my arm.

"Hey, for what it's worth, the sister was nuts. I had a long talk with Jacobs and he said all indications are that she was an emotional train wreck. Not only that, but she was manic one day and near rock bottom the next. Even with your talents and skills, you couldn't have known she was going to blow her head off."

Talents and skills, I thought. *How dulled were those attributes on that day? How many indicators did I miss because of the cloud in my mind?*

"I know," I said. "Thanks."

We resumed walking and as we got closer to the house, we could see it was even larger than it had first appeared.

Chase asked, "What do you call this type of house? A villa?"

"I'd call it expensive," I replied.

We moved up a series of stone steps and onto the porch. Chase dug in his pocket and withdrew a single key.

"The manager of the housekeeping crew left the key with Homicide. Needless to say, the sister never asked for it to be returned."

He unlocked the deadbolt and we stepped into a grand foyer. I hadn't exactly expected there would be a party going on, but for some reason the silence bothered me. It took me a moment to realize why. There was no alarm panel beeping, warning us that we should enter a code into the system.

"No alarm?" I asked, as if Chase should know.

He shrugged and searched along the walls until he found a plastic covered panel.

"He had an alarm, but I guess his service expired. I doubt any of our guys would have had a code to set it after they cleared the scene."

It occurred to me that all of Jimmy's utilities had probably gone unpaid as well. I flipped a light switch and confirmed there was no electricity.

I said, "The front gate must be on a separate line or, more likely, emergency power."

Chase pointed to the right and said, "Jacobs told me the recording studio is back there somewhere."

I knew from the media reports that one of the housekeepers had arrived for work and found Jimmy Spartan's naked body in the middle of the studio. The official cause of death was blunt force trauma to the head, and detectives determined the fatal blow came from a weighted microphone stand. As I'd mentioned to Jimmy's sister Tracy, cocaine had been found on the body, but drugs had not contributed directly to his demise.

The hallway we followed darkened as the number of windows decreased. Eventually we reached a room that was nearly pitch-black and I realized my stupidity at not bringing a flashlight since the light on my phone wasn't going to provide much illumination. I was both relieved and a little irritated when Chase pulled a flashlight out of a holder on his belt and clicked it on.

He made a tsk-tsk sound before saying, "What kind of PI doesn't have a flashlight?"

I rolled my eyes. "I'm not a PI, at least not officially. If I ever get my license, I'll start carrying one."

"And tell me again why it is you haven't taken care of that little detail?"

I ignored the question, gestured toward the dark room and said, "Would you mind leading the way? I need the big cop to protect me from the scary people."

Chase chuckled and slid though the doorway. I trailed him into the windowless room and the beam of his powerful Maglite crept slowly along the walls. Acoustic foam lined nearly every inch of wall space. Chase twisted the top of the flashlight to create a beam with a wider radius and then I noticed a series of musical instruments were staged in various locations in the studio. At one end of the room was a booth where I assumed a sound engineer would push a thousand buttons and turn five thousand dials in an effort to get a perfect effect.

"Here's where the body was found," said Chase, directing the beam to the floor. "The mic stand was right over there." Chase moved the beam to a location several feet away from where Jimmy's body had fallen.

A section of the hardwood floor showed traces of discoloration from Jimmy's blood. As I'd expected, there were no visible traces of the powdered cocaine that had been found on his body. The crime scene techs would have diligently collected those items.

I asked, "Can you shine the light on the instruments?"

Chase did and I wasn't surprised to see fingerprint dust visible on nearly every flat surface of a musician's tools of the trade. A yellow bass guitar leaning against a stand was now covered with the dust, as was an acoustic twelve-string that had once had a natural wood finish. A Gibson Les Paul cradled by a silver stand had been dusted and still sat in the corner of the room. The drum set was mostly black, but the white drum heads had been searched for prints as well.

"There had to have been a ton of prints found in this room," I said. "Jimmy had his band record here sometimes. He used to record at a famous studio in Memphis, but his last few albums were recorded right here in this room."

Chase gave me a quizzical look.

"Did the sister tell you that?"

I shook my head. "No. I read it somewhere." I said as I stepped over to the drum set and let my fingers slide along a cymbal.

"Now I get it," Chase erupted, laughing.

"What?"

"You're a Jimmy Spartan fan," he said, pleased at his deduction. "That's why you're working this case."

"I was hired," I reminded him.

"By a dead woman," he said. "You could pocket that money and walk away. Or, you could donate the money to charity if you were so inclined. But, you've decided to snoop around because you're one of Spartan's Warriors."

At the mention Jimmy Spartan's fan club, I shot Chase a look.

"Nobody calls his fans Spartan's Warriors anymore. He's famous, but hasn't been a major act in twenty years. I doubt most people under the age of thirty-five could even name one of his songs."

"But, I bet you can," Chase taunted. "I bet you know all of the songs. Did you have big hair and leather pants back in the day?"

Taking the flashlight from his hand, I walked over to the window of the sound engineer's booth and shined the light through the glass.

"They dusted in there too," I said. "Since no arrests have ever been made, I'm guessing the prints the techs recovered didn't lead to anything substantial."

Giving me a brief reprieve from his hair band harassment, Chase filled me in on the few details he knew.

"They identified the prints of the sound engineer, Jimmy's regular band, plus a couple of stand-ins who helped with certain songs. Apparently, they had finished recording a new album and the three band members had scattered across the country to work on other gigs. Two of them had minor criminal records, so their prints were in the system. The third guy, the drummer, was at home in Louisiana and voluntarily submitted his fingerprints through New Orleans

PD. It was a moot point, because each one of them cooperated fully and supplied solid alibis for the time of the murder. It doesn't look like any of them were in the state at the time."

Chase paused and corrected himself. "Well, the drummer's alibi wasn't exactly rock solid. He said he couldn't remember what state he was in on the night of the murder. In fact, he couldn't be one hundred percent certain he was in the U.S. at the time. But, there is a YouTube video of the lucky bastard sitting on a boat in the Gulf of Mexico, doing tequila shots off some swimsuit model. The New Orleans cop who interviewed him for us, said the drummer is about as bright as a box of hammers and probably would have confessed to the murder by accident if he'd actually done the deed."

I shook my head and said, "There's a club on the South Side that has a sign that reads, 'Drummers must be accompanied by an adult at all times.' Maybe there's something to that."

Chase chuckled and said, "From what I heard, it took about a week to track all of these guys down. Fortunately, due to Jimmy's fame, other departments around the country were eager to cooperate."

I was sure he was right. If not for the Jimmy Spartan name, it likely would have taken much longer to convince other busy jurisdictions to lend a hand on a murder committed in the Keystone state. If we were in a police drama on television, each of Jimmy's closest associates conveniently would have lived and worked inside of the Pittsburgh city limits. In real life, many people—especially musicians— have transient lives.

"What about the sound engineer?"

"Local kid," Chase answered. "Roger Orta, but goes by the name 'Stretch.' He was at his apartment with his girlfriend and she alibied him. It may not be the most trust-worthy alibi, but there was no indication of bad blood be-tween him and Jimmy and nothing tying him to the crime. I've got his information out there in my car."

I pivoted around the room.

"Which way was the body facing?" I asked.

"According to Jacobs, it appeared Jimmy was near the center of the room and facing the door we just walked through when the killer swung the mic stand and hit him in the back of the head. So you might say the killer did a mic drop."

I ignored the joke, "So the body fell forward?"

"Right. One big blow to the back of the head and then lights out. From the blood splatter and the samples found on the mic stand, it looks like the killer was standing fairly close to the drum set when he dealt the blow."

I asked, "How tall was the mic stand?"

"I'm not sure," said Chase. "But you would assume it would be at mouth level. So, four to five feet? Maybe short-er if someone was sitting while using it. The base was heavy and round, so it took some strength to swing the thing."

I said, "I read that there was no sign of forced entry and no alarm activation recorded. I didn't notice any cameras on the way in, so I'm guessing there's no video."

"That's what I was told," Chase stated. "The M.E. puts the time of death between nine and ten p.m. There were lines of coke set up in Jimmy's bedroom, so a working theory is that he was up there snorting when he heard something downstairs. He made his way to this room, and somehow the perp gets behind him and chops him down," Chase concluded while making a left-handed chopping motion.

Something about Chase's movement sparked something inside of me. I let my head drop and allowed my eyes to go out of focus. In my mind, the room transformed and eventually was clear of fingerprint dust and bloodstains. I was in the studio, but not here and now. It was the night of the murder and a naked and high Jimmy Spartan is coming through the doorway. Reflexively, he reaches over and flips the light switch next to the door, illuminating the studio. His head moves side-to-side, his expression curious but not overly-alarmed. A worried homeowner grabs pants or a robe before searching his home for an intruder, but Jimmy wasn't particularly concerned.

Jimmy walks into the room and, not immediately seeing anyone, searches the only two hiding places around. He steps over and peers through the glass of the sound booth and then pads over to the drum set. He sees the intruder, his eyes widen and he says something before turning to leave. Before he makes it more than a couple of strides, the killer grabs the mic stand and takes a wide-arching backswing. But, not the way Chase had imitated doing so.

"Trevor," said Chase sharply, bringing me back.

"He had to have taken the swing right-handed," I said. "Given the position of the body and the proximity of the drums, the killer wouldn't have had the space to take a left-handed backswing. The killer would have had to have taken a step in this direction," I said as I paced over to a spot several feet away from the drums, "before he could have space to take the swing. By that time, Jimmy would be halfway to the door. There's no way Jimmy would have turned his back on a random intruder unless he was running full speed. It doesn't make sense."

"Trevor," Chase said once again.

I turned toward him. "What?"

"You know damn well what."

"I'm fine," I assured him.

"No. You're not fine. You're off your meds and doing that thing you do."

He was talking about what I call my "blur-outs." Those are moments when I'm able to mentally insert myself into a crime scene like a witness. It's nothing supernatural or anything. I just have the ability to tune out everything but the facts of a case, while being able to access parts of my brain where I've perceived things that may not have been clear to me at the outset. This ability was invaluable to me during my career in law enforcement. The problem is that after my abduction by a drug gang made up of gangsters from various Eastern European countries, I started having hallucinations. Fortunately, the affliction is treatable with the right medication. However, I've found a side-effect of the meds is that I can't concentrate worth a damn and blur-outs are completely impossible.

"It's under control," I told Chase.

He snatched the flashlight out of my hand and stormed out of the room. I stood there in the darkness and wondered if Jimmy Spartan had really surprised an intruder, or if he'd turned his back on someone he knew.

TRACK 3
"PICTURE IMPERFECT"

I made my way back to the grand foyer where a Chase was leaning against a wall. His body language told me he was fuming, but I knew there wasn't much I could do to cool his anger.

"You're an idiot," he observed.

"It's temporary," I said, meaning I'd be back on my meds in no time.

"No, it's not. You're always an idiot."

Touché.

"Damn it, Trevor. We've both seen what happens to people who don't get treatment for PTSD. Even the ones who never experience a hallucination struggle to adapt. You can't do this to yourself."

I walked over and leaned against the same wall.

"I can't work cases if I can't concentrate," I said.

"You don't have to work cases," he spat. "You could…"

There was a pause while he tried to come up with something. Anything.

"Get high?" I suggested.

He gave me a sideways glance.

The anger dissipated from his eyes and he said, "Look, I get it. You need a puzzle the way you needed a fix. I'm just not sure replacing one addiction with another is the way to go."

We stood in silence until he said, "Are you seeing a shrink?"

"Yes."

"Is it helping?"

"I don't know," I said truthfully.

"Are you going to keep this up?" he asked. "Are you going to keep working cases?"

"Until I figure out what else to do."

"Why haven't you gotten your PI license?" he asked.

I shrugged. He moved away from the wall and paced.

"Is it because it would mean you are acknowledging you aren't ever going to be a cop again?"

One of the things I loved about Chase was his brilliant analytical ability. One of the things I hated about Chase was his brilliant analytical ability.

"Something like that," I replied.

He processed my words and then jutted his chin toward the front door.

"Let's get out of here," he said.

"Not quite yet," I said, while pulling out my cell phone. "I want to walk through the house and take some photos."

He looked at me incredulously and said, "The *entire* house?"

"It shouldn't take long," I lied. "It will help me get a better feel for the victim."

Chase sighed, but handed me the key to the house.

"Call me when you're done, so I can get that back."

I thanked him and he strode to the front door and pulled it open. I rocked off the wall and stood straight when I saw the two men waiting on the porch. One had the build of a bulldozer, a shaved head, and tattoos peaked over the color of his brown leather jacket. His partner wore a gray hoodie and long black hair peeked out of each side of the hood and fell over the drawstring holes. Upon seeing me, the bulldozer spoke excitedly to his partner in a language that sounded like Russian or Czech. Although I didn't recognize these two, I had no doubt as to their cause and their intentions. The organization I'd damaged had decided the time was right to get their revenge.

With my right hand, I reached for the gun concealed on my back. My heart raced and my gut tightened when my fingers found nothing but air. My gun was concealed all right. It was concealed in a desk drawer in my house. Not my best decision this week.

Realizing Chase was about to become collateral damage in a war he never wanted, I opened my mouth to yell for him to draw his weapon. The sound stuck somewhere in my chest when Chase walked right between the two heavies without giving them a second of attention. It was as if he'd never even seen them. Then, I knew he hadn't and he wouldn't.

Chase turned back to me and said, "Don't break anything. I don't think anyone in Homicide will be snooping around here, but I'd rather avoid any uncomfortable questions."

He must have noticed something in my face because he said, "Are you okay?"

"Yeah," I responded while swallowing hard. "Thanks for this. I'll call you when I'm done."

Chase closed the door behind him and pulled it until I heard a loud click. Beads of sweat had formed on my forehead and I wiped them away with one hand.

"That's why it's better if I'm not carrying a gun," I mumbled to myself.

After I spent a few minutes calming down, I navigated the house and took photos in each room. By all accounts, nothing had been taken when Jimmy Spartan had been bludgeoned to death in his studio. The housekeeping staff and a few close friends had looked through an assortment of photographs and nothing seemed out of place. Still, I knew that a killer doesn't enter a home intending to murder someone without having a plan and a weapon. The mic stand was a weapon of opportunity, not a sign of premeditation.

When I'd finished, I locked the front door, called Chase and met him in a parking lot north of the city. I handed over the key and let him chastise me about my medical condition for a few minutes. When he ran out of steam, he reluctantly handed me a folder. Back at the house he'd said he had some information in his car, but this was more than information. It was the entire case file, including interview notes and autopsy results. I knew he could find himself in hot water if anyone found out I'd been given a copy. He sped off before I could thank him, so I headed home. I checked my rearview mirror, but my imaginary friends were nowhere to be found. However, I figured some manifestation of my condition would reappear soon enough.

Since it was the middle of a weekday and most people were working actual jobs, traffic was light as I made my way to the neighborhood of Brookline. As I pulled up to the curb, I gazed at my house through the driver's side window of my Volkswagen Jetta. After seeing a rock star's mansion inside and out, my timeworn house looked like something out of a documentary about The Great Depression. I put the car in park, grabbed the case file from the passenger seat, and went into my ill-furnished abode.

I synched my cell phone to the computer in the living room and started uploading the photos I'd taken earlier. While I was tempted to dive into the case file, I opted to go for a five mile run. I'd been a runner before the abduction that had sent my life into a freefall, and now I was doing my best to get back into the habit. Not only did running help me clear my mind, but I'd discovered it helped me fight off some rather unhealthy urges that involved me putting a needle in my arm.

The terrain of Brookline challenged my legs, and my chest heaved as I crested the first hill. While I sorted through the information in my head, I periodically glanced back to see if my fictional shadows were in pursuit. Of course, I knew the hallucinations couldn't cause any real harm, but I was still relived to find I wasn't being watched by anybody—including myself.

As I approached my house, I slowed my pace to a walk and let the wind cool my face. My University of Akron sweatshirt was soaked, so I stripped it off the second I was in the door. After a quick shower, I wrapped a towel around my waist and caught a glimpse of myself in the bathroom mirror. I knew the man staring back at me was not yet forty-five, but he appeared much older. Life had taken a toll on me early in my fourth decade, but it seemed nature had pressed the pause button over the past two years. Although I still had no wife, no kids, no stable employment, and only one friend—who currently believed me to be an idiot—I'd been having a relatively decent stretch. But, that had been a medicated stretch.

I tossed on a pair of jeans and a maroon long sleeve shirt and headed downstairs to read the case file. Sitting at my kitchen table, I spent thirty minutes skimming through official reports, case notes, forensic analysis findings, and crime scene photos. Everything was as Chase had explained, including the weak alibi provided by the sound engineer, Roger Orta, a.k.a. Stretch. Contact information listed him as living in an apartment in Highland Park. I've always liked approaching witnesses and suspects cold—not calling them ahead of time—so I decided I'd stop by his place later that evening.

Then, I moved into the room that I reluctantly refer to

as my office and checked if all of my photos had uploaded to my computer. It appeared everything had worked properly, so I grabbed a glass of water and put the images I'd downloaded on one of the two monitors that were hooked up to the computer. I started clicking my way through the dozens of photos I'd taken that morning and I was about a third of the way through when I realized the pointlessness of the exercise. With nothing to compare the photos to, I was grasping at straws. Then, it occurred to me that there might be a way to compare photos from before the murder to the ones now in my possession.

I did an internet search for a television show titled *Celebrity Abodes* and pulled up its website. After Jimmy Spartan's death, a cable station had launched a series of promos around an episode of *Celebrity Abodes* filmed at the Spartan house in Pittsburgh. The original episode had been aired months before his death, but the network executives had decided to dust it off to capitalize on the media attention his death had received.

I'd remembered seeing the commercials and wondered if perhaps it had been archived online. The full episode wasn't, but I found a tab titled *Photo Albums* on the *Celebrity Abodes* website and clicked on a hyperlink with Jimmy's name. In seconds, a slideshow popped up on my screen and I realized I was looking at a picture of the front gate Chase and I had passed through hours prior. Small font in the corner of the image told me I was looking at photo one of fifty-two.

Keeping the slideshow up on one of the monitors, I moved the window containing the photos I had taken over to the other monitor. Now I could do my best to compare images captured months ago by the television crew to the ones I'd taken this morning. While I wasn't expecting to find anything conclusive by doing this, I figured it couldn't hurt.

Other than the occasional object being in a different spot within a room, it appeared the house had remained much the same between the day of the filming and this morning. The larger pieces of furniture hadn't been moved and it appeared chairs had been moved no more than one would expect. The studio was an exception as the instruments and mic stands were in different locations. This wasn't surprising considering Jimmy would have used the studio to test out and record new ideas and would have touched every instrument. It was no secret Jimmy Spartan, a brilliant songwriter, had the ability to play multiple instruments and had recorded his first single entirely on his own.

The story, which was now legendary, was Jimmy had saved up for months to buy some recording time in a studio. He then went on to record each component of the song separately by playing guitar, bass, drums, and then recording the vocals. From that point, he worked with the studio to piece the components together and he used that single as a demo and ended up with a record deal within the year.

As I sat in my office and compared the two images of Jimmy's home recording studio, I thought about how painful the early Alzheimer's diagnosis must have been for the man. For him to bear witness to the deterioration of his own incredible abilities had to be intolerable. I couldn't begin to imagine the frustration and anger he would have felt if he had known his record label had turned down his latest creation.

With a few more clicks, I arrived at photos of what could only be called a game room. When I had stood in that room earlier in the morning, I had marveled at the collection of electronics and collectibles Jimmy had accumulated over the years. Along walls that had been painted bright red, stood lines of pinball machines and arcade games. A billiard table took up one section of the floor, while a Skee-Ball machine and an air hockey table occupied another. One wall seemed to be the home for nothing but high-end sound equipment, including speakers that nearly reached from floor to ceiling. Everything was orderly and, I assumed, pricey.

Other than a few billiard balls I suspected had been strategically placed about the green felt table for the television production, nothing was different between the two images I was inspecting. I was about to move on when something caused me to freeze. I focused more closely on the wall of sound system equipment and my eyes darted from one monitor to the other as I mentally divided the screens into quadrants. Jimmy seemed to have every musical medium covered. A stereo that included a cassette player, a deck capable of playing CDs, a docking station that appeared to be for an iPod or other digital player, and even an 8-track player. I systematically picked apart every aspect of the images until I reached the bottom right corner.

In the photo from the television production, something stood at what appeared to be knee level. The stand appeared to be little more than a table that might be used for a small television and VCR, but the stand appeared to hold two rectangular boxes, the top one silver and the one below it green. The silver box had knobs and switches on the front panel and appeared to be topped by a black disc and metal arm. I glanced back to the photo I'd taken. There was no stand and no devices. Nothing.

The format of the image used by Celebrity Abodes didn't allow me to zoom in on the photo, so I leaned in and squinted for a while before it occurred to me I was looking at a record player. I searched my memory for everything I remembered about record players, which took no time, since I remembered very little. While I owned one that I never used, it was small and basic, not like the one in the photo. I didn't remember seeing the player anywhere else in the house, so had he given it away? Sold it? Tossed it out with the trash? I had no idea and knew it probably wasn't important. Additionally, the odds of the record in the photo being *the* record were slim. However when you're grasping at straws, you don't throw any back for being too small.

From the angle of the photo, I couldn't tell much else about the record player. But, I knew someone who would. The wonderful thing about trying to find someone who is knowledgeable about a dying medium is that there is a limited amount of people to approach. In Pittsburgh, that list consisted of one name. If you wanted to buy a record player, sell a record player, or have a record player fixed, you went through Vince Sonta. I decided I'd make a quick stop on the way to meet Stretch the sound engineer. I knew Vince held an encyclopedia's worth of information in his head. I just had to hope he didn't hold a grudge.

Planetary Electronics was wedged into a line of shops on Murray Avenue in a portion of the city called Squirrel Hill. I wasn't able to find parking on Murray, so I turned up Phillips Avenue and drove on the red bricks until I found a spot and then walked back to Murray and waited to cross the street. Hoping I wouldn't have to wait for the crossing signal, I looked left and then tried to peek right to see if any cars were coming down the hill. I leaned out and craned my neck, but a white van parked to my right blocked my view. While I was pulling back to the curb, I noticed the van rock ever so slightly. Dutifully, I waited for the signal before crossing and once I'd made it to the opposite sidewalk and started walking up the hill, I glanced back at the van. A magnetic sign on the side of the van read *Sochacka Plumbing Services* and listed a local phone number. I gritted my teeth at reading the name and cursed under my breath when I saw a silver sunshade covered the windshield. Since Sochacka was the last name of one of my now-incarcerated kidnappers, I realized it was a not-so-real version of him was stalking me now. Interestingly enough, my hallucinations had learned how to drive.

Outstanding.

I reached the doorway of Planetary Electronics and walked up a narrow staircase. Moving past a doorway leading to an adjacent record store, I shuffled through a hallway until I found Vince's workshop. The scents of vinyl, wood, and composites no longer manufactured in this country penetrated my nose the second I crossed the workshop's threshold. Shelves holding old stereos extended the length of every wall and glass counters contained newer pieces of equipment. I looked around, but I appeared to be alone in the shop. I spotted a silver counter bell situated next to a sign reading *Ring Bell for Service,* so I did while contemplating the irony that an electronics store didn't have an electronic bell of some sort.

"Be with you in a second," boomed a voice from a back room.

A few seconds later, a sturdy man in his fifties emerged from a doorway while cleaning a pair of eyeglasses on a tissue. He looked up at me, squinted, and then put on the glasses.

He stopped in his tracks. "Detective Galloway."

I tried to weigh his tone, but couldn't tell if he sounded resentful, apprehensive, or noncommittal.

I put both of my hands on the glass counter in front of me and said, "Hello, Vince. How are you?"

He moved one shoulder up and down in a half-shrug and lumbered over to the opposite side of the display case.

"It's been a long time," he said.

I noticed he didn't seem to be giving indication he wanted to shake hands, so I didn't make the attempt.

"About four years, I suppose."

"Five," he responded tersely.

A long moment passed before I rolled the dice by asking, "How is your brother?"

Vince glanced away and I thought he might either walk away or lunge over the counter and wrap his monstrous hands around my throat. Instead, the tension in his face seemed to lessen.

"He finished doing his bit in Rockview a few months ago. He's on parole and working at a car dealership. He's doing okay now."

"Good," I said before there was an awkward pause.

He took in a deep breath and let his eyes meet mine. The rest of the tension left his face and he said, "Look, I know it was nothing personal. You did what you had to do and you believed me when I told you I didn't know he was dealing out of here. I admit I was mad at first, but it was Greg's stupid decision to get involved with that ecstasy stuff."

I nodded. "I know I misled you, but I didn't have much of a choice in the matter."

Vince smiled for the first time and said, "Hell, part of me was mad because you were a good customer. Well, at least Sean Watkins was. I had no idea you were a cop, and obviously you fooled Greg."

I didn't know what to say. I'd used the persona of Sean Watkins to become a mainstay in the shop and cozy up to Vince and Greg. The PD wasn't going to let me use official funds to buy electronics, but Vince sold records in the adjacent room. I bought dozens of albums in a short period of time and developed a faux friendship with the brothers. Greg had a reputation for dealing party drugs and once he'd become comfortable with me, I'd made a few buys from him. When I'd arrested him and confiscated his stash, he'd rolled on his supplier and testified in exchange for a reduced sentence. Some in my department had wanted to get the Feds involved, try to make a case against Vince, and seize the shop. Ultimately, I made a convincing case that Vince had no knowledge of his brother's crimes and Vince and the shop were left alone.

"It was the job," I said.

Vince's expression became puzzled. "*Was?* Aren't you still a detective?"

I shook my head. "Retired on disability. I'm private now."

"Oh," was all he said.

"But, I could use your help with something."

His eyebrows raised and he said, "Well, I was going to say you look like you're here on business, but you never were exactly the smiling type." He grinned. "Okay, what can I do for you?"

I started to speak, but turned when I heard footsteps behind me. A bearded man in his early twenties shuffled into the shop and around the glass display case. In spite of the season, he wore baggy cargo shorts and I could see a sizable brace on his left knee. The brace wasn't the flexible elastic bandage sort. It was metal, sturdy, and had a look of permanence.

The man started to scoot past, but Vince touched his arm and said, "Tom, do you remember Detective Galloway?"

Tom?

I couldn't believe this was the same scrawny, clean-shaven, seventeen-year-old kid I remembered from my days as Sean Watkins. The scruffy man in front of me was thirty pounds heavier and from the looks of things, most of that weight was contained in his biceps. If not for the skinny legs and the limp, he'd have looked like college wrestler.

Tom Sonta stuck out his hand and we shook.

"Did Uncle Greg do something again?" he said without emotion.

"Not that I'm aware of," I said. "And it's not detective anymore. Just call me Trevor."

He gave a nod and turned to his father.

"I dropped off the GE to Mr. Sullivan and he said he's going to bring two more record players by next week. He has an 8-Track player he wants you to look at too, but he thinks it might be beyond repair."

Vince raised an eyebrow. The act makes me jealous because I would love to be able to manipulate my facial muscles in that way. Although with my stoic mannerisms, I doubt I would capitalize on having such a gift.

Tom, catching his father's look, held his hands in the air and said, "His words, not mine."

He pulled a set of keys out of a pocket of his cargo shorts and tossed them to Vince. The shorts were one thing that hadn't changed with Tom. No matter the weather, I'd never seen him wear long pants. He adjusted a flap on his shorts while shuffling his way between tables covered with components and oddments and then disappeared into the back room.

The breaks of a city bus squealed from outside a large window. Vince waited for the sound to soften before directing his attention back to me.

"I didn't encourage it, but Tom decided to join the family business," Vince explained. "He handles most deliveries and goes out to do simple repairs on large items that are hard to transport. He's become invaluable to me."

"What happened to his leg?" I asked in a way that sounded more indelicate than I had intended.

Vince walked around the counter, went to the window, and stared down at the hill I had just ascended. I took a spot beside him and glanced down at Murray Avenue. The traffic was buzzing. The people on the sidewalks were buzzing. The hallucinated plumbing van my brain had created was sitting in the same spot. Just sitting there.

"It happened right down there last August," Vince explained, pointing. "Tom was going to pick up lunch at the Cuban place that used to be over there. You remember that place?" Vince closed his eyes and said, "Damn. What was the name of the restaurant?" He repeated the question while making a rolling motion with his hand, as if that would prompt the memory to hurry along.

"Adelmo's?" I asked.

"No, you're thinking of the Salvadorian joint that was there before that."

"Estiban's?"

"No, no. That was the Argentinean place that shut down in 2009."

"Adolfo's?" I said.

He opened his eyes and snapped. "That's it. Adolfo's."

The memory of the business was coming back to me. "Now I remember. Didn't the owner die and the daughter didn't want to take over running the business?"

Vince nodded as his memory refreshed as well. "Yeah, yeah. The poor guy had heart attack right there in his kitchen. Died on the spot."

He'd been a burly guy with black curly hair. I could still see him coming out from the kitchen and talking to all of the lunch guests, which had on occasion included me. He seemed to run a tight ship and got rave reviews in the local papers for the authentic Cuban cuisine he'd supposedly brought over from homeland.

"There have been a lot of good food joints in that spot," Vince observed. "I just wish they would last."

"He was a nice man," I said. "What was his name?"

"The one who owned Adelmo's?"

"No, the other one."

"Estiban's?" asked Vince.

"No, the other one."

"Adolfo's?"

"Yeah," I confirmed.

"Stan," laughed Vince. "He grew up in the South Hills, didn't know a lick of Spanish until high school, and probably couldn't find Cuba on a map. But, man did that guy know how to cook."

We nodded in agreement and watched another bus struggle to slow as it approached an intersection, the driver burning the brake pads on the steep grade.

"Anyway," Vince resumed. "Tom didn't walk down to the crosswalk, but walked out between two parked cars. The downhill lane had been clear for a moment and Tom stepped out. A Nissan that had been parked a few spaces up from where Tom was crossing saw the same gap in traffic that Tom had, pulled out, and hit the gas. It was some guy doing the same thing we've all done at one time or another in this city. So, he clipped Tom with the front bumper. The kid was lucky it was just a knee and a slight concussion. It could have been worse."

Vince sighed, gave his head a quick shake, and turned to me. "Why are you here, Trevor?"

"Record players," I said.

The big man let one corner of his mouth rise and said, "Why do I have a feeling you aren't looking to buy?"

"Because you're smart."

"Why do I have a feeling you're blatantly flattering me to get cooperation?"

"Because you're really smart."

He laughed and waved at me to proceed.

Before I'd left my house, I'd used my phone to pull up the

Celebrity Abodes website and located the photo in question.

"I'm interested in this right here," I said while pointing to the object with the silver and green components. Without being able to zoom in on the photo, it was little more than a speck in the corner of my Smartphone.

Vince leaned in and I said, "It's hard to make out, but here in the corn—"

"What does Jimmy Spartan have to do with this?" Vince interrupted.

I turned the phone toward me and scrutinized the photo and the page text. There was nothing on the screen identifying the location.

I asked, "You've been to Jimmy Spartan's house?"

"No," he said. "But I certainly recognize that Telefunkin PS81DD."

I nodded knowingly. I waited for more. And I waited.

"Well, yeah," I said with a healthy dose of sarcasm. "Obviously you noticed that."

Vince didn't even flinch. He was never great at catching sarcasm. After another ten seconds of the two of us staring at each other, I said, "Vince."

"Yeah?"

"What in the name of God is a Telefucking R2D2?" I asked with all the patience I could summon.

Vince's eyes widened in genuine surprise. Over the years, I've had this happen from time to time when dealing with a genius in a specific field. I'd had conversations like this before with Vince—conversations in which he honestly doesn't realize the scope of his knowledge and the depth of others' naïveté.

"Oh, the turntable you were pointing to. The one in the corner."

I glanced back at the phone and asked, "How can you possibly identify the type of record player from this photo?"

"Turntable," he said.

"What?"

"It's a turntable. A record player has speakers built in as part of the unit. What you showed me is a turntable which requires that speakers or headphones be attached in order to hear what is playing off a record."

"Right," I sighed. "How do you know that kind of turntable? Have you been around one before?"

"Yes," he said. "But, just that one. They are very rare. Only a handful of them around."

"You worked on *this* one? You worked on the one Jimmy Spartan bought?"

"No, but I helped him get it," Vince answered. "He understood that I know all the serious sellers and collectors and can locate hard-to-get items. He didn't want to randomly search the internet and end up buying a piece of junk. So, we contacted a foreign collector I occasionally deal with, helped negotiate the price, and arranged for delivery. The seller sent the item to us in the usual manner. Jimmy was more than satisfied when he took possession. In fact, I'd say he was thrilled."

I rubbed a hand through my hair and realized I needed a haircut.

"Do you know if he sold it, or maybe sent it back?"

The big man's brow furrowed. "No. Why?"

"It's not in his house anymore," I told him.

"I don't believe Jimmy would have sold it, and you know I'm the man to see if a unit that valuable needs any repair work."

"How much did it cost?" I asked.

Vince hesitated and winced.

"He's been dead for months, Vince. I don't think he'll mind."

He still didn't budge, so I said, "His sister hired me to

45

look into his murder."

"The sister who killed herself? Tom saw something about it in the newspaper."

"Yes. That sister."

From his expression, this seemed to generate more questions, but he eventually said, "Six. He paid six, plus the costs for shipping and labor. He threw a little extra my way for helping him out."

I thought about the total cost of the turntable, the shipping, and Vince's cut and said, "So...what are we talking about? He paid maybe a fifteen hundred for everything?"

During the previous thirty seconds, I must have grown another head. At least that's how Vince was looking at me.

"Six thousand. Jimmy paid six thousand for the turntable alone." Then, as if I didn't understand—which I didn't—he added, "It was in remarkably good condition."

While that kind of money was a drop in the bucket for Jimmy, I still couldn't wrap my head around the price tag.

"I think the one I have in my living room cost me about fifty dollars," I said.

"Well, you get what you pay for," he told me.

"I mean no offense, but why would anyone pay six thousand dollars for a record player?" I asked.

"Turntable," Vince corrected again.

"Sorry."

His chest rose and fell in exasperation as he explained. "It's a true collector's item. Very few of the PS81DDs were made and while it's unknown how many are still out there in working condition, I'd bet less than ten. You may not know this, but while Jimmy had a wild rock star side he truly appreciated music and all of its mediums."

"So, the rec...the *turntable* made records sound better?"

"Not necessarily," Vince replied, pushing his glasses up his nose. "But to an ear as discerning as Jimmy's, it's possible."

I paced over to the window again and thought about what I'd learned. If Jimmy Spartan was truly happy to have received the turntable and it was working properly, then there would be no reason for him to sell it or throw it out. It was possible he put it in storage somewhere, but why would he? Even with the hefty price tag of the turntable, there was much more expensive equipment lying around the house.

"Do you have a piece of paper?" I asked Vince.

He went behind the counter and fumbled around a desk for a moment. He returned and handed me a Post-It note. I pulled a pen out of my pocket and jotted down my number.

Handing the paper to him, I said, "I know it's a long shot, but can you call me if you hear of anyone trying to sell the turntable?"

He seemed indecisive and for a moment I thought he was going to ask for money. Thanks to television, everyone thought cops and private investigators handed money to informants left and right. It happens, but not as often as one might think. But it turned out Vince wasn't looking for a financial angle. Something else was on his mind.

"No card?" he asked.

"What?"

"Don't you have a business card? On TV, all the PIs dish out business cards and say things like, 'If you hear anything through the grapevine, shoot me a call.'"

"Sorry. I ran out," I said.

I started to leave but turned when I heard Vince say, "Hey, Trevor?"

"Yeah."

"Take it easy on yourself, okay?"

It was an odd thing to say, even for someone as eccentric as Vince.

My eyes must have revealed my confusion, because he explained, "I know it's only been five years, but you look like you've aged ten."

Vince was never much on keeping up on current events, so while my ordeal with the drug gang was major news in Pittsburgh, I wouldn't have been shocked if he had no knowledge of those events, the toll they took on my physical health, or my subsequent addiction.

"Just wear and tear, my friend. Wear and tear."

As I crossed the intersection of Murray and Phillips, my thoughts were on a dead rock icon and a rare turntable that was apparently missing. Later, I'd check with Chase to make sure the PS81DD wasn't sitting in some evidence room because a crime scene tech thought he found something unusual and decided it needed processing. Or, maybe somebody got clumsy at the scene, knocked the thing over, and decided to make a piece of broken equipment disappear. Hell, for all I knew, Jimmy had bought the turntable as a gift and now it was sitting in his guitarist's living room.

All of these thoughts were nipping at my cerebral cortex, which is probably why I hadn't noticed the individuals nipping at my heels. Hearing the scrape of shoe moving a pebble on brick, I turned to see a pair of men who could have been close cousins of the hallucinations I'd seen at Jimmy Spartan's house. If fact, at first glance I wasn't certain they weren't the same two I'd manufactured that morning. While lost in thought, I'd walked right past the Sochacka Plumbing van and hadn't given it a second glance. I guess this pissed off my imaginary friends, who certainly like attention.

"Not now, guys," I said before turning away and taking another step toward my car.

Now, I've learned a few things about my hallucinations over the past few years. They make sounds. They change clothes. They talk, they walk, and now I knew they could drive. But, there was one thing I'd never, ever noticed in all the times I'd interacted with my mental specters. I'd never seen one cast a shadow. Not once.

So, after I'd turned my back on the pair and glanced down at the bricks scrolling beneath my feet, you can imagine my surprise when I saw the shadow of and arm raising up toward the back of my skull. And while I don't have a degree in Shadow Interpretation, it doesn't take genius to recognize the outline of a handgun. To me, the shape of the gun was almost as distinct as the sound I heard next.

The sound of the shot sent shockwaves through my body and I ducked, turned, and spun before I realized that I should have been amazed that I still had the ability to duck, turn, and spin. The two men were in a full sprint and one was holding a wounded shoulder. The pair zigzagged and then darted out of sight between two houses. I tensed as I saw two more people running my way. One was a young man whose hair and build screamed military. The other was a woman, and she was also holding a gun. I relaxed a little and tried to get my heart rate to slow. It was possible the woman wanted to end my life, but not because of my previous undercover work. If she did want to end my life, it was because at one point she had loved me.

TRACK 4
"ALWAYS A WOMAN"

"Turn around, put your hands behind your back, and don't say a word, Trevor."

I did as I was told and didn't struggle while she put the cuffs on me. She'd put them on a little tighter than necessary, but from the fire coming out of her eyes as she'd approached me, I thought better than to mention my discomfort.

"Walk" was all she said as she guided me in the opposite direction from which she'd come, which had been the intersection with Murray Avenue.

The man with her had his gun drawn and was scanning the area, keeping an eye out for my would-be assailants who, it seemed, were pointedly less imaginary than I'd initially thought.

She pushed me into an alley and I immediately noticed there were no cars parked in the narrow passageway. I had assumed I was about to be tossed into the back of a car before being whisked away, but now I had no earthly idea what was happening.

"Jackie?" I said quietly.

When we were halfway down the alley, she spun me around hard. "What the hell are you doing?"

Her companion was watching the mouth of the alley

and from the way he moved I had no doubt he'd be able take care of any threats that might appear.

"What am *I* doing?" I said. "I was walking down the street when—"

"When we saved your ass," she interjected.

"Right," I said. Then, I started to understand what had happened. "Did you fire the shot? Did you hit that guy in the shoulder?"

She took a breath and said, "Yes."

Our eyes met and the fire in hers seemed to lose some heat.

"Thank you," I said. "I never saw those guys coming."

The hardness in her expression eased and I was reminded of her beauty. She wasn't a fake *Cosmo* type of beautiful, but more of what my father would have referred to as a firecracker. Standing five feet, five inches tall, with jet-black hair and an athletic build, Jackie Fontree had all the 'S's.' She was stunning, sensual, and sophisticated. She also happened to carry a few more S's around, because she was a Special Agent with the U.S. Secret Service.

I asked, "Are you okay?"

She cocked her head, some of the fire returned to her eyes, she leaned in close and exclaimed, "Am *I* okay? Am *I* okay?"

My investigative instincts were telling me she might not be okay.

"Because of you, our surveillance operation may be blown and, now that I've shot someone, I'm going to be staring down the barrel of an administrative suspension pending an internal investigation."

That's another problem with television and movies. People think law enforcement officers go around town getting in gunfights and never get taken off the street while being investigated for discharging a firearm. In real life, once you fire your weapon your own agency, the media, and the general public put you under a microscope. It can be easy for the facts to become subject to interpretation to those who have political motives. Even a cut-and-dry shooting like this one could turn into quagmire. Not to mention, her surveillance operation was probably blown.

Surveillance operation?

Now I realized why there was no car for them to toss me into. Jackie and her partner had come running from the intersection I'd just crossed a few seconds before. Therefore, they had to have been set up at a relatively stationary location near the corner of Phillips and Murray. A location...like a plumbing van that could be parked on the street each day for weeks at a time and people would assume one of the local businesses had a large project that required a plumber. Perhaps a plumbing van with a sunshade in the front, to keep any nosey pedestrians from peering into the vehicle.

"That was you in the plumbing van," I said.

She ignored me and shouted to her partner while digging her cell phone out of a jeans pocket. "Nick. I'm calling it in. I'm going to have a car sent over to where Douglass Street meets Shady Avenue and they can get Galloway to the field office. We're going to be tied up giving statements for a while, so I'll see if Moreland can get another team to slip in the van after seven."

So, they *had* been in the van. I thought about the location, the way the van was facing, the small tinted windows that would allow for visibility on only a few locations. I stared at Jackie. She dialed her phone and then put it up to her ear.

"You're watching Planetary Electronics!"

She grimaced and said, "Damn you, Trevor. I hope I can salvage this."

Speaking into the phone, she said, "It's Jackie. I need to

talk to Moreland."

She took a step away from me while waiting for this Moreland to get on the line. I figured Jackie would only have to wait a few seconds before they tracked him or her down. I'd been in the Secret Service's Pittsburgh Field Office before and knew it wasn't particularly large.

Jackie, having never been one to waste time, made the most of her few seconds of being on hold by saying, "Trevor?"

I looked at that firecracker face. Until that moment, I hadn't realized how much I'd missed her. Even now, I could still count on her.

"Yes," I said.

"You've gotten old."

I suddenly remembered why it's wise to stand away a safe distance after lighting the fuse of a firecracker.

If you visit nearly any doctor in the United States, the chances are you will find yourself in a bright examining room that has a sterile ambiance that includes the scent of antiseptic potpourri. Interrogation rooms are pretty much the opposite. The one in the Secret Service's Pittsburgh Field Office was musty, complete with drop ceilings composed of water-damaged tiles. If I were to venture a guess, none of the millions of dollars the agency received in appropriated funds had been spent on my lopsided folding chair which, if the carved-in graffiti was to believed, had once been occupied by "Jay Rock." Unlike what one sees on television, there were no two-way mirrors built into any of the walls. However, a rectangular box next to the doorway that was supposed to look like a thermostat, but was probably a camera. Not coincidentally, the chairs and the table in front of me had been angled in such a way that the "thermostat" would have a nice shot of my face but wouldn't be blocked by anyone sitting directly across from me. I looked up and did more inspecting of the ceiling tiles until I saw the tiny microphone positioned above the table. The room was small and was feeling smaller by the second. At least the agents who had brought me to the Washington Place address had been kind enough to take the cuffs off me once I was in the chair.

The door opened and two people entered who couldn't have contrasted more. The first was a lean African American man who wore a suit that seemed to be molded around his frame. The second was a woman wearing ripped jeans and a baggy flannel shirt. Her brown hair dangled down past her shoulders, down the front of the shirt, and terminated at the Pittsburgh Police badge that dangled from chain around her neck. After an attempt on my life, I'd been handcuffed, yelled at, tossed into a car, placed in an interrogation room, and now both the Secret Service *and* the Pittsburgh cops wanted to speak with me. I didn't want to be oversensitive about the whole thing, but for some reason I doubted this was the typical treatment for the victim of a crime.

"Mr. Galloway, my name is Ken Moreland. I'm the ASAIC of this office."

So, Jackie had called the Assistant Special Agent in Charge of the office who would logically be monitoring their operation from afar. He didn't make any attempt to shake my hand, confirming my "victim" status was questionable at best.

Moreland stepped to the side and said, "This is Detective Angie Michael. Pittsburgh PD sent her over here to take your statement about what happened today."

"Okay," I said. "Somebody tried to kill me and Special Agent Fontree saved my life."

Neither of them moved. Neither of them smiled. I suspected neither of them liked me.

Detective Michael grabbed a pen and a notepad from her back pocket, pulled out one of the chairs on the opposite side of the table, and sat. Moreland stayed in place and conveyed no desire to take the last vacant seat in the room.

"We've never met, have we, Trevor?" asked the detective in a way that told me she knew I had once been in her shoes.

"No," I replied. "How long have you been with the department?"

"Six years. I was on patrol until last year."

"Then we overlapped a little, but I've been gone a while," I said. "What zone did you work?"

"Two for the final fourteen months. Zone five before that."

"Busy areas," I said.

She nodded and let herself smile. "You get a lot of good experience, but you know how it is. You've been there."

"Sure," I said.

"My last sergeant was Stoddard. You probably know him, right? He's been around a while and did some time in investigations."

I leaned forward and said, "Angie."

"Yeah."

"It's not that you aren't good at it, but why are you trying to build rapport with me? Somebody tried to kill me. Cooperation is in my best interest."

I was genuinely curious, but my words had come across as confrontational. It was the story of my life. Now, her smile was gone and Moreland's demeanor...well, it couldn't have gotten any more stone-like anyway.

"I'm sorry," I said. "That came out wrong. I simply didn't want you to put out a lot of effort to try to get me to talk. I'm willing to talk. I want to talk. I don't know much, but I'm an open book. Ask away."

She scowled at me, clicked the pen, and put it the paper.

"Fine, Mr. Galloway. Let's get to it. What were you doing at Planetary Electronics?"

"I can't tell you."

Needless to say, my inquisitors were less than impressed with my response and I was on the receiving end of their withering stares. I'm not sure how things went for Jay Rock when he sat in that chair, but I wanted to leave or maybe climb under the table. After another thirty seconds had passed, I was pretty sure even the table wanted to get under the table.

Again, I hadn't intended to be adversarial, but I had been expecting them to question me about the attempt on my life. When they started asking about Planetary Electronics, I defaulted to private investigator mode and thought about confidentiality. As the stares became more intense, I realized that argument was never going to fly. First, I wasn't a licensed private investigator. Second, there is no such thing as court-recognized PI/client confidentiality. But, if I told them the truth, I would either be warned off my case or charged with obstruction. I decided my open book approach would be a work of fiction. It wouldn't stand up to scrutiny, but it might get me out of the room.

"Just kidding," I said. "I have a CD player that's broken and I wanted to see if Vince Sonta could fix the thing."

Michael and Moreland seemed unconvinced, but Michael started taking notes.

"A CD player," she said.

"Yes. I came across it recently and plugged it in, but it wouldn't play. I asked Vince if he thought he would be able to get it working."

"From what I understand, you weren't carrying any CD player when you entered the building and your hands were just as empty when you left," said Moreland from his standing position.

"I was in the neighborhood, remembered about it, and dropped by to ask Vince what he thought."

Angie Michael put her elbow on the table and rested her chin in her hand. "Why were you in the neighborhood?"

"Lunch," I said. "I was on my way to have lunch."

"Where?"

"The Italian place on Forbes."

"Isabella's?"

"Yes."

"I've been there," she said. "They make the best calzone."

"That's true."

"The owner is nice, too," she said. "But, I can't remember his name."

"Luther," I said. "Did you know that in a previous life he was a state trooper."

"You're kidding," said Detective Michael. "I never would have pegged him as a cop."

I said, "And he played minor league baseball before that. He's an interesting guy. The next time you're there ask him—"

"Excuse me," boomed Moreland, stepping closer to the table. "But, maybe we can talk about why one of my agents had to shoot somebody today. Or, should we all head over to Isabella's and see if this guy Luther wants to weigh in?"

Michaels sat up in her chair and got back to the matter at hand. "So, you went to Planetary Electronics and talked to Vince Sonta about fixing a CD player. Then what happened?"

"I was walking back to my car and two guys appeared behind me. One of them raised a gun, but Jackie shot and wounded him."

"*Jackie?*" Moreland asked.

An uncomfortable silence found its way into the conversation before I said, "Agent Fontree."

Moreland leaned over and put his palms flat on the table. "You know Agent Fontree?"

"Yes."

"How do you know her?" he asked.

"We dated for a while."

He sighed. "When did the two of you stop seeing each other?"

"A couple of years ago."

Moreland stood and stepped back from the table. I knew what he was thinking. Shootings of any kind get media attention and even the slightest impropriety can trigger a media feeding frenzy. If word got out that an attempt had been made on the life of a former police detective and he had been saved by his courageous ex-girlfriend who happened to be a Special Agent with the Secret Service, the lights from the cameras would be blinding. Any hope for keeping their Squirrel Hill surveillance operation secret would die the death of a thousand journalists. Moreland looked worried and I knew it was because he was seeing all the angles and few of them worked in his favor.

Detective Michael noticed the tension and chimed in. "But, you don't have a relationship with her anymore? What I mean is, are the two of you still friends?"

"Our relationship ended badly."

"How bad?" she asked.

"You should probably polygraph her and ask her if she was shooting at me," I remarked.

She laughed. Moreland did not. I didn't show it, but I was getting a little irritated by the fact that nobody seemed to be overly concerned that someone had tried to kill me in broad daylight.

"You haven't asked me for a description of the two men who ran up on me," I observed.

"I was getting to that," said Michael. "Go ahead."

I gave what little description I could. Honestly, I hadn't paid much attention to the details at the time since I thought the two were fashioned by the misaligned part of my mind.

"Had you ever seen these men before?" she asked.

"No. But Jackie—Agent Fontree said she saw them following me before I went into Planetary Electronics."

"But, you didn't notice them?" she asked.

"No."

Detective Michael put down her pen and placed both of her hands in her lap. "Mr. Galloway, none of this makes any sense."

"You can ask Agent Fontree and her partner. That's what happened."

"No, I get that," she said. "But, *your* actions don't quite line up."

"I'm not sure what you mean."

Her head turned ever-so-slightly and her eyes shifted toward Moreland. I got the impression that whatever she had to say, she would have rather the two of us been in private. However, she continued. "After we started talking, you asked why I was attempting to build rapport with you."

"Right. Like I said, I didn't mean any offense. I was saying—"

"I wasn't doing it because I consider you any kind of suspect," she interrupted. "I was doing it because I've heard all about you and what happened before you left the department. I guess it was my way of trying to let you know that I don't harbor any ill-will. Nobody could have withstood what you went through and I don't think much of those who do the chest pounding and condemn you for breaking under those circumstances. The truth is, when they teach us about your ordeal during in-service training, the lesson has nothing to do with resisting torture, it's all about not being taken captive in the first place."

My stomach turned, but I tried not to show my discomfort. "They use me as a case study? I'm an annual training requirement?"

She shifted and joined me in feeling uncomfortable. "I'm not explaining it correctly. They use your situation to explain the importance of officer safety and to describe how bad things can turn out if you—"

"If you don't follow procedure," I said.

Michael's expression was one of empathy. Even Moreland, who probably didn't know the entire story looked less indifferent to my well-being.

"Something like that," said Michael.

Not wanting to go any further down that road, I said, "What about my story doesn't make sense to you?"

She visibly became more comfortable as she slid back into the familiar role of interrogator and said, "First: Who gets a CD player fixed anymore? Who even *owns* a CD player these days when everything is digital? And if someone does have one, it's going to cost more to fix it than to buy a new one off eBay."

She had a point, but I was ready with a reasonable response. "I have a million CDs at home and I don't want to upload them in to my computer and then transfer them into my iPod. The only time I really listen to music is when I'm home, so rarely use my iPod."

"Okay, let's assume that's true. That still doesn't explain how a former narcotics detective who was once taken prisoner doesn't notice he's being shadowed by two men who are somehow able to get the drop on him."

"I'm rusty," I said.

"And calm," she said. "Less than two hours ago, you went through a traumatic experience and your hands aren't even shaking. You look as if you're a few deep breaths away from falling into a meditative state. Somebody was about to put a gun to your head."

"I'm aware of that."

She raised her eyebrows. "You're aware."

"I'm aware."

She turned to Moreland and shrugged. "He's aware."

Moreland walked back to the table and said, "The man you talked to inside Planetary Electronics. Vince Sonta, right? Are you two friends?"

"Not really, but we know each other."

"How?" he asked.

"I put his brother in prison for dealing."

Michael and Moreland looked at each other in disbelief. Then Moreland said, "So, what you're saying is that you were looking to get a CD player fixed by a man whose brother you once arrested, and then you—a former cop—didn't notice two men who were looking to rob or kill you until your federal agent ex-girlfriend saved you by shooting one of the suspects?"

I nodded.

Moreland threw his hands in the air and said, "I can't go with that story. Even a watered-down version sounds implausible."

Detective Michael looked at nothing in particular, tugged on her hair and I heard her tapping a foot under the table. Then she stood, faced Moreland, and gestured to the door.

She said, "Let me talk to you for a minute, Ken," and the two of them walked out of the room.

Twenty minutes passed before they returned. This time, Moreland took the chair across from me and Michael remained standing.

Having recaptured his expression of stone, he said, "Here's what we're going to do..."

61

TRACK 5
"COMPLICATED"

"How did it make you feel to see her again?" asked Dr. Welch.

This was typical of the way she asked questions of me. Here I was sitting on the couch again, detailing how two Eastern European drug gang enforcers tried to take me out, and she's focusing on the fact I saw Jackie again.

"Considering she saved my life," I began. "I'd have to say I was relieved."

She stared at me with those eyes and her lips began to form that addictive smile. The psychiatrist crossed her endless legs. Her skirt was shorter today. If I didn't know any better, I'd think she wore it just for me. Her favorite patient.

"Were you happy to see her?"

I put my arm up on the back of the couch and it sunk into the cushion as if it had always belonged there. "Aren't we going to address that my paranoia is looking a lot more like valid situational awareness? The last time we spoke, you voiced some doubts that I was actually a target."

Her body swiveled, but the chair remained still. "Would you mind answering my previous question before we discuss the attempt on your life?"

I let my arm slide down the couch and rubbed my eyes. It was getting late.

"I liked seeing her," I admitted. "It's been several years since we broke up."

"You mean, since she left you because of your use of heroin and displays of erratic behavior?"

It wasn't really a question, so I didn't bother responding.

"Did she enjoy seeing you again?" she asked.

I shrugged. "I didn't see her after she and her partner walked me down the street and stuffed me in a sedan. Two other Secret Service agents took me to the local field office where I was questioned by an agent and a Pittsburgh detective. Whatever it is they are working in Squirrel Hill, they didn't want anything as minor as the attempted murder or a former narcotics detective messing up the surveillance operation."

Dr. Welch asked, "I would assume the sound of gunfire and involvement of federal agents probably did that anyway, correct?"

I shook my head. "They came up with a cover story for the press. They are releasing a statement that a couple of agents with Homeland Security were having lunch and happened to spot a robbery in progress. If asked, I'm expected to corroborate the story."

"Will you?"

"Yes," I replied.

"Why?"

My head ached. I needed to sleep and then get up and go for a run. I needed to clear my head.

"Trevor. Did you hear me?"

"Because," I said. "It's the right thing to do."

I stared at the clock on the wall and watched the second hand tick an orbit around the center. The hand struck each second so hard, so decisively. But if you looked carefully, you could see the hand vibrate at the conclusion of each second. It was slight, but it was there. As if things weren't so decisive after all. As if each approaching second was not in fact a foregone conclusion.

"That's a lie," she said, bringing me back into the moment.

"Excuse me."

Her dazzling smile was gone and she was leaning forward. I could see cleavage protruding from her blouse, but being accused of lying was distracting me from being distracted.

"You aren't going along with the story for any noble purpose. You're doing it because it's practical."

I crossed my arms and then, realizing how defensive it appeared, uncrossed them.

"You didn't tell them why you were at Planetary Electronics, did you?"

"Not exactly," I said.

Dr. Welch pointed a finger and said, "You're an unlicensed PI who was hired by a dead woman to investigate a case the police couldn't solve. You're bending, if not breaking, the law and you know you're likely to step on some toes. You're going along with their cover story because you think you may need their help later on when you're sitting in a prison waiting to go to trial for obstruction of justice, operating as an unlicensed private detective, and whatever other charges they feel like pursuing."

"Jail," I said.

"What?"

"Jail. I'd be in jail, awaiting trial. In most places, prison is what you call the place you are sent after sentencing and even then they only send you there if you have a year or more to serve. Most people don't understand the distinction."

"Trevor."

"The call the jail in Butler County a prison. I'm not sure why."

"Trevor," she said with growing impatience.

"Yes."

"I think you get my point."

"I do," I said. "Sorry."

She straightened up and gathered herself. "You can't stand on a trapdoor and expect someone will be there to catch you when it opens. You, as well as anybody, know this to be true."

I did. Nobody was there to catch me when I had been abducted and tortured. For weeks, I endured whatever they dished out until I broke and gave up every bit of information I could remember—the names of undercover detectives, informants, operational details...everything.

"Are you going to try to see her again, Trevor?"

Swinging to from one topic to another with the subtlety of a wrecking ball was another tactic Dr. Welch enjoyed.

"I don't know," I said honestly.

"Do you want to?"

"I don't know," I said dishonestly.

We sat for a few moments listening to that clock tick away.

"Yes," she said. "You were right. It seems there are people who still want you dead."

There was something odd in her expression, but I couldn't quite get the meaning.

I said, "To be honest, I was starting to have doubts myself. But, I guess I'm not quite as crazy as I thought."

There it was again. That expression. It was something beyond solemnity. It was a decisive seriousness, but with a trace of an uncertain vibration at the tail end. That second hand vibration was...it was fear.

"Doc," I said. "I'm going to be more careful. As soon as I make some headway on this case, I'm going to be back on the pills."

This only made her expression go from dusk to midnight.

"I'm concerned," she said.

"I can see that."

"I'm not only concerned for your safety, Trevor. I'm concerned by the fact that you radiate a sense of validation because the threat against you is real and not in your head."

I leaned forward and said, "I'm not sure what you mean."

She mirrored my pose and explained, "In the past, you've exhibited self-destructive behavior on a grand scale. I fear you may be taking risks as a substitute for other damaging behaviors. You are working a case that nobody cares about and walking around completely exposed when you can't distinguish a legitimate threat from one that is not real. But what bothers me most is that I can see you are finding some level of comfort in knowing the attack on your life today was real. In essence, you may be feeling more secure as your existence becomes less secure. To continue on this path may produce a volatile situation."

Another silence filled the space between the two of us.

Finally, I said, "I don't think I want to hurt myself. Not consciously and not subconsciously."

She let her eyes drop to the floor and then pulled them back up to meet mine.

"An addict is an addict, Trevor. Whether the drug of choice is an opiate or an investigation, a small dose usually leads to a big need. If you choose to move forward with this case, you may have to ultimately decide if justice for a life already lost—Jimmy Spartan's life—is really worth the one you are living now and the one you could have in the future."

The clock on the wall ticked and ticked and ticked.

The doorbell woke me at eight. I slid out of bed, threw on a pair of sweatpants and stumbled groggily toward the sound.

The house had gotten cold during the night and I wrapped my arms around my shirtless torso as I approached the door. Realizing I needed to start answering the door with my gun at my side, I debated turning back and grabbing it from my bed stand. Before I could decide what to do, a voice I recognized penetrated the old wooden slab separating me from the outside world.

"Wake up and open the damned door, Trevor!"

I did.

"Good morning," Jackie.

I didn't remember doing it, but in my sleepy condition I must have invited her to come inside because that's exactly what she did.

I closed the door and stood there naked from the waist up. She surveyed the surroundings and was either reminiscing about the good times we had once had in this house, or checking to see if I had become a slob.

"At least you still keep the place clean," she observed.

So much for reminiscing.

With hard eyes, she asked, "Are *you* clean?"

"Don't beat around the bush," I said sarcastically. "Just ask me whatever you want."

She put her hands on her hips and waited. I noticed her gaze dropped to my arms, which were still crossed over my chest for warmth.

Realizing what she was doing, I extended both my arms with the underside of my forearms exposed and said, "No new track marks."

She swallowed and said, "Oxy?"

I shook my head and said, "I'm not on anything."

I opted not to mention that I wasn't taking my medication either.

She seemed to be weighing my answer and then said, "Okay."

"Okay," I said. A few beats passed and I asked, "Do you want some coffee?"

She walked over to the couch and sat down. Dressed in old jeans and a Carnegie Mellon University sweatshirt, she could have been settling in to read the newspaper and do the crossword. But, I knew those days were gone.

I went back to the kitchen, started the coffee pot, and then went back to the bedroom to get dressed and brush my teeth. After a few minutes, I returned to the living room with two mugs. She thanked me and sipped as steam rose around her smooth features.

I took a seat beside her and adjusted so we could face each other. We didn't speak for a while and I realized my surprise at seeing Jackie had turned to joy, and now that joy was transforming to sorrow. With her sitting inches from me, I was once again reminded of all I'd thrown away.

Understanding the fragility of the situation, I was afraid to speak. A couple of times I opened my mouth, but then simply took a drink from my own ceramic mug. I reminded myself not to rush anything. I had all the time in the world. The only thing I had planned to do today was find Roger Orta, Jimmy's sound engineer. Thanks to my little side trip to see Vince the day before, I'd never made it to Orta's Highland Park apartment.

"What were you doing in Squirrel Hill yesterday?" Jackie asked quietly.

"Like I told your colleagues, I wanted to ask Vince about fixing my CD player."

She watched my face, but my expression held. I suppose that's one of the advantages of being stone-faced ninety-nine percent of the time. You get a lot of practice.

"And where exactly is this CD player?"

Damn.

"It's broken. So I put it in storage."

She pursed her lips, nodded and said, "Sure, because this house is so cluttered with you living here by yourself."

Damn.

I thought I was going to have to attempt a quick recovery, but then her resolve broke.

"I...you...you do live alone, right?"

It wasn't there long, but it was there. She was afraid my answer might be "no."

"I'm alone," I said. This was true if you didn't count the cerebral boogeymen that tended to pop up.

An ounce of relief appeared on her face and she sipped self-consciously. "Trevor, are you involved in something illegal?"

What? Why in the world would she think that?

"No," I said. "Why—"

"You used to have a habit to support. Did you get in too deep with somebody?"

"No," I said. "I've been clean for a while. I still get checks from the city and I have a little saved up."

Remembering how I'd let my addiction ruin us and how I'd lied to her while trying to cover up my failures, I decided not to lie any longer.

"I'm working a case," I said. She looked up. "That's what I was doing in Squirrel Hill."

She nearly spilled some of her coffee.

"For who? What agency?"

"For a private citizen," I said. "I was hired to snoop around an old case."

"You're a PI?" she asked, seeming a little happy about the fact I was employed in any capacity. "Why didn't you say so?"

"Technically, I'm not a private investigator. I'm not licensed or anything."

"Why not?" she asked.

"I don't...I guess...Well, Chase thinks that I haven't accepted that I'm not going to be a cop again and having a PI license would be admitting I'm through."

Jackie smiled. "Chase has always been extremely smart. I miss him."

"You could have stayed in touch with him after we broke up," I reminded her. "I wouldn't have minded."

She tilted her head as if she'd considered this at one point in the past. "No," she said. "I needed a clean break." Her expression saddened. "You just hated yourself so much. You hated yourself to the point the hatred bled out of your pores. It bled onto me."

"I'm sorry," I said. "I am so sorry. It may not matter to you anymore, but I have changed. I may be all out of hate for anything or anybody, including myself."

She inhaled deeply, put her mug down on the coffee table, and stood.

With more steel in her voice, she said, "You still hate yourself, Trevor. You haven't changed that much."

"What are you talking about? You don't know—"

"You had to have known there are people out there who want you dead. You were the one who told me years ago that you may never be safe from these guys. I watched those two men stalk you while you walked up to the electronics store."

It was starting to dawn on me that the pair had to have tailed me from my house and then waited for an opportunity to make the kill appear like a robbery-gone-bad. I hadn't noticed the tail at all. Not good.

Jackie continued the barrage. "Then, I watched in amazement as you walked down the street and *still* didn't pick up on the fact you had shadows."

I didn't speak.

"But that's not really the case, is it, Trevor?" she said.

I wasn't certain where this was going, so I waited.

"In that alley, you told me you never saw those guys coming."

"Right," I said. "I know I should have been more—"

"You talked to them," she yelled. "Trevor, I saw you turn and say something to them. Then, you turned your back to them and acted like they were no more of a threat than a puff of smoke."

I had no answer for this. At least I didn't have an answer I thought she could handle at that moment.

"It's complicated," I said.

"It's complicated? No. It's not complicated. You're numb to your hatred because you're suicidal."

"I'm not suicidal," I asserted.

"Really? You weren't armed yesterday and today you answered your door without a gun. That's not the man I knew. Where is the fight in you? Where is the man who got kicked out of VMI because of his temper?"

My short stint at the Virginia Military Institute occurred long before I'd met Jackie. The two of us got to know each other while working on a cross-jurisdictional task force, but once we had become romantically involved I'd told her of my less-than-honorable dismissal from the school.

"I'm learning to control my anger," I explained.

She began pacing the floor as she continued. "One of the things about me that drove me nuts was that sometimes you seemed to be at the point of boiling over. Now, there isn't any heat coming from you at all. It doesn't have to be all or nothing, Trevor."

I pivoted to watch her while she strode back and forth.

"Are you getting professional help?" she asked with concern.

"I talk to a therapist."

"Does it help?"

I sat down on the couch again and said, "I think so."

Jackie leaned against a wall and she slid her hands into her pockets.

With the topic of *me* having run its course, she asked, "What are you investigating?"

"An old homicide," I replied.

"What homicide?"

I wasn't sure why, but suddenly I was reluctant to continue with this all give and no take part of the conversation.

"What are you working?" I asked.

She seemed to resent my dodging her question and said, "What harm is it to tell me whose murder you are working? What does it matter?"

"It probably doesn't, but I'm curious why you were set up on that corner."

She moved away from the wall and stepped into the center of the room.

"Trevor, what are you working?"

"I told you, it's an old homicide. Nothing that falls under Secret Service jurisdiction. What are *you* working?"

"Hey, I'm on administrative suspension for saving your life," she fired back. "I may be riding the bench for a week or more because of the shooting. Not to mention, I've been sitting in that Sullivan Plumbing van for weeks and we still don't know if our surveillance is blown. The least you can do is talk to me about your case."

Technically, the *least* I could do was to keep my mouth shut but now was not the time to split hairs. It took a few seconds, but something she had said finally registered in my mind.

"You mean Sochacka Plumbing," I said.

"What?"

"You said Sullivan Plumbing. You meant Sochacka."

"Trevor, what in the hell are you talking about?"

Confusedly, I asked, "You were in the white plumbing van on the corner, right? The one with the sunshade over the dash."

"Yes," she said impatiently.

"The magnetic sign on the side read, Sochacka Plumbing, not Sullivan."

She cocked her head and squinted. "Look, we've used that van for various operations over the past two years. I'm the one who decided we would be Sullivan Plumbing for this assignment. I don't know anything about that other name."

My eyes wandered the room. Not only could I not be sure what people were standing in front of me, but I now knew words and names from my past were creeping in from the periphery. Without the meds, my condition was possibly degenerating faster than ever before. Not good.

"Now tell me about your case," she said again.

I put my mug down, rose from the couch, and stepped toward her. "I'd be happy to. You go first," I demanded.

"Are you seriously going to withhold information from a federal agent who saved your life?" she yelled. "Are you crazy?"

I wasn't sure if that was a rhetorical question, so I let it pass.

The volume of my voice raised a decibel or two as I said, "I'm just interested in knowing why the Secret Service, that has a somewhat limited jurisdiction to financial crimes and threats against those it protects, is camped out on the corner of a nice neighborhood. I'm a concerned taxpayer."

"You're being an unreasonable jackass."

"I'm being totally reasonable." I said, not arguing with the jackass part.

She muttered a curse, threw the door open, and stormed out, slamming the door behind her.

I watched that door for a long time. I wanted it to open

and wanted it to stay closed. I felt her presence and felt my loss. I hurt at having lost her so long ago and felt hope for having seen her again. But, I felt something else deep inside. When we had been arguing, an old friend had peeked around an emotional corner. For a few seconds, I had felt anger. I had felt anger and it felt good.

Maybe the frigid Tin Man had a little coal left in the furnace after all.

Roger Orta's Highland Park apartment building sat on a tree-lined section North Negley Avenue. The fall breeze made colorful leaves dance across the street and on the hood of my car as I brought my Volkswagen to a stop along the curb. Before getting out of the car, I reviewed the info in the folder that had been provided, albeit illegally, by Chase. I hadn't noticed the first time I'd read the file, but apparently Orta's nickname, Stretch, was ironic. At five-foot-six, he probably wasn't working in the music industry as a side gig while he pursued a career as a professional basketball player. No photos of Orta had been included with the file, but being thirty-two years old and one hundred ninety-five pounds, I was guessing he was either a bodybuilder or a little soft around the middle.

After Jackie had marched out of my house, I'd gone on my computer and run a search on Orta's address. The street address had come back to a Wellesley Manor Apartments and, after a little more digging, I learned the rates for the units ranged from twelve hundred to fifteen hundred dollars per month. I had no idea what kind of salary a good sound engineer made, but it seemed Stretch was doing all right.

I got out of the car and wandered around until I found the main entrance. A locked door and a wall of buzzers told me I wasn't going any further on my own, so I ran my finger down the line of buzzers until I found one lining up with the name R. Orta. I glanced at my watch and noted it was a few minutes before nine. I wagered that if he was home at all, then he was probably awake. I pressed the buzzer.

"Yeah."

I pressed the *talk* button next to the intercom. "Mr. Orta?"

"Who's this?"

"Hi. I'm a detective and I was wondering if we could talk for a minute. I'm a friend of the Spartan family."

By using the title of "detective" I wasn't saying I was a cop, but I wasn't saying I wasn't a cop. A lengthy pause. I wondered if I'd pressed the button hard enough.

Sounding irritated, the man said, "What do you want?"

In the kindest voice possible, I explained, "Jimmy's family asked me to check on some things. You were close to Jimmy, so I thought you may be able to help. I'm kind of at the end of my rope and I don't want to go back empty handed. I'd really appreciate it if we could talk for a few moments. I won't take up much of your time, sir."

I thought that sounded okay, assuming he didn't know Jimmy's sister had killed herself and was Jimmy's only family. I hadn't sounded accusatory or pushy. Just a guy trying to help out the family. A friend of a friend, really. Hoping to have a friendly chat to keep everyone happy. I'd even tossed in a 'sir' to give him the feeling of being the authority figure. In all modesty, I'd have to say I played it perfectly.

There was a slight hum coming from the intercom and I could tell the button had been pushed from his end. Three seconds passed before he spoke.

"Fuck off."

Huh.

If this had happened to me a few years ago, I probably would have pushed buzzers until somebody let me in, stomped up to Orta's apartment, and then had a rather severe conversation with the man while showing flashes of my trademark temper. But, private citizen Trevor Galloway was not going to do anything of the sort. The new me took a deep, cleansing breath and returned to my car. I drove the car around the corner to where I had a nice view of the main entrance and there I sat. I could do this because I had an advantage over the old me. Private citizen Trevor Galloway had nothing else to do and nowhere else to go. Jimmy Spartan wasn't going to get any more dead. Unless I employed the services of a medium, my client wouldn't be requesting any progress reports from me. I had no real job, no significant other, and no circle of friends waiting for me to show up for brunch. But I had time. I had lots and lots of time.

Noon came and went and I had started to wonder if I'd missed Stretch leaving his apartment. Of course, I had no idea if he was still working as a sound engineer or if he held down any other jobs. I assumed if he was still in the music business then he might keep irregular hours. If so, being locked in his apartment at lunchtime on a Wednesday might not be unusual for him.

I sat slouched in my car for a few more minutes and then decided I'd risk swinging through a drive-thru for some food and then return to my observation post. I turned on the ignition and straightened up in my seat, quickly checking the rearview mirror out of habit. A pair of coal-black eyes stared at me from the back seat. They blinked one time.

With my right hand, I reached for the gun sitting on my hip underneath an untucked shirt. Because of the attempted attack in Squirrel Hill, and Jackie's admonition, I'd decided to risk carrying the Sig Sauer 9mm. I began a clumsy attempt to spin in my seat, but drawing a weapon from my right hip and twisting in the same direction made the maneuver all but impossible. Suddenly I stopped, realizing that in spite of my poor tactical positioning and having been taken by surprise, I had one distinct advantage over the adversary breathing down my neck. I was alive and he wasn't.

I froze and listened to him breathe. My gaze stayed fixed on the rearview mirror and I watched the eyes blink again. The expressionless, weathered face was framed by greasy hair that stopped an inch above shoulders covered by a dirty denim jacket. Years ago, I'd shot and killed Lukas Derela after I'd tracked him to the cheap motel where he had been hiding. A few months prior, I had been reinstated after having been rescued from captivity and torture. Derela was the only member of my captors who was on the loose and an old informant had tipped me as to his location.

The last night I had seen Derela alive, I had slid my unmarked car into the dimly lit motel parking lot and moved in without calling for backup. Instead, I walked into the room and put three rounds in his chest. Officially, it was a clean shoot since he had come at me with a knife. Unofficially, I wasn't sure anymore. The incident left enough doubts in the minds of department officials that I was invited to take a disability retirement and vanish, which is what I did. Regrettably, Lukas Derela seemed to have little difficulty finding me whenever I was off my meds.

"You need to go," I said to him. To myself.

The black eyes disappeared behind his eyelids and then reappeared.

"Our account is settled. I've got nothing left for you."

Slow breaths.

I peered into the mirror. Into those eyes.

"You took my life too," I said. "But, you did it slower." Breaths.

I waited for him to leave, but he sat motionless.

After nearly half a minute, he spoke. The voice was akin to a hiss. The sounds emerging from his body could have been gasps of oxygen escaping a lonely corpse.

"Mistake," he said. It said.

Motion from under the mirror caught my attention and my eyes refocused long enough to see Roger Orta walking beside a woman in her twenties. The two strode down a sidewalk and got into a red Lexus IS 300, a forty-thousand-dollar car if purchased outright. The two of them chatted while Orta slid into the driver's seat and the woman got in the other side. Having missed my chance to approach Orta on the street, I decided I needed to follow him and make another run at him whenever he got to his destination. Unfortunately, I was traveling with some extra baggage.

I shifted back to the mirror, but saw nothing but the street laid out behind me. Slowly turning around, I found I was alone again in the car. I inhaled and smelled gunpowder that I knew was not actually hovering in the air. I exhaled and felt dread. Fighting your enemies is hard enough. It's significantly more difficult when you don't know which ones are real. When one of those enemies is *yourself*, the odds are decidedly against you.

I buckled my seatbelt, put the car in drive, and followed Roger Orta. I didn't know if he would be an enemy or an ally, but I knew two things for sure. He was alive and real. Those facts gave me a sense of relief few can understand.

Orta weaved the Lexus through the city for the better part of forty minutes, eventually arriving at a collection of shops and restaurants called Southside Works. He lucked into finding a parking spot on Sidney Street and I had to drive past him in search of my own. I double parked at the end of the street, turned on my flashers, and leapt out of the Jetta. I did my best to hurry back toward where Orta had parked, while trying not to look like I was rushing. By the time I came up to the Lexus, it was empty. I scanned the area and spotted Orta's backwards cap move through a crowd toward a theater. Luckily, he was a Dodgers fan. If he would have been wearing a Pirates or Steelers hat, I'd have had absolutely no chance of spotting him in this city.

I swung around the corner and caught up to Orta and the girl who were holding hands and seemed to be just another happy couple catching a matinée. They slowed as they approached the entrance, and I kept moving forward since Orta had never seen my face. He opened the door for his significant other and she walked inside. He looked back and studied the pedestrian traffic, myself included, for a moment and then moved through the doors.

I'm not sure why, but I choose not to go after him and make another attempt at stating my case for why he should talk to me. Instead, I would lay back and watch him for a while. Seeing no purpose in sitting in a theater with the lovebirds, I walked past and then doubled back to my car. I snatched a parking ticket off the windshield, crumpled it up, and threw it inside the car. After moving my car to a legal parking spot, I grabbed my black leather coat out of the back seat and strode over to a pub I'd seen while following Orta. I asked the hostess for an outside table.

"It's a little chilly out here. Are you sure you want to sit outside?" asked the hostess who was wearing a thin T-shirt much more suited for indoors.

"I'm sure," I said.

"All right," she huffed as she picked up a menu and led me to a metal table.

I sat and made sure the spot I had picked had a clear view of Orta's Lexus. Feeling satisfied with my choice, I put my arms on the table. It wobbled and I noticed someone had unsuccessfully attempted to level the table by placing sugar packets beneath the legs. I added a couple more to the collection, but it did little to stop the movement.

A waiter approached and I ordered a sandwich, fries, and a Coke. I figured I had at least ninety minutes before the movie finished, so I got as comfortable as one can get on a rigid chair and I wrapped my jacket tight around me. My food arrived and I was a few bites into the meal when I surveyed the area and did a double-take. Orta was moving toward his car. Not only was he moving, but he was alone and moving fast. He seemed to be looking everywhere as if there was a threat right behind him. Before I could react, he squealed away from the curb and was gone. Realizing I had no chance of catching up to him, I sat and thought while sipping my Coke through a straw.

Inspecting the area, I saw no reason for Orta's urgency. I saw no reason to not finish my sandwich. Since I knew where he lived, I could try to catch up to my new friend Stretch anytime I wished. But, after ten minutes I did see a reason to leave my table. The girl who had been with Orta was standing near the parking space that was now occupied by a Chevy, not a Lexus, and threw her hands up in disbelief. Even from a distance, I could read confusion and then anger on her face. It appeared my man Stretch had left his date without a ride. Fortunately, I had a car and plenty of time.

TRACK 6
"BROKEN COMPASS"

"Is something wrong, miss?"

She spun my way. I timed my arrival for when she was putting her cell phone into her pocket. I couldn't hear everything she had been saying, but I surmised she was leaving an angry voicemail for Stretch.

"You seem upset," I said. "Is everything all right?"

Her knee length coat flapped to her sides and now I could see she was rail-thin and wore a black shirt with the word VOLBEAT printed across the chest.

"I'm fine," she huffed as she started to walk away.

"Have you ever seen them live?" I asked quickly.

She looked at me perplexed.

"Volbeat," I said. "I saw them play when they were in town a few years ago. I love their music."

She examined me with obvious skepticism and adjusted her black knit cap, leaving visible only a few locks of blonde hair.

"Oh yeah, what album is your favorite?" she asked, testing me.

The truth was, my favorite album was one of their more recent ones, but I gave her the name of the band's lesser-known first record to show I was for real.

"That's old school," she said approvingly.

Hiding my disappointment that a twelve-year-old album was "old school," I nodded.

Acting as if I was breaking off the conversation, I made a quarter turn away from her and said, "Anyway, you seemed distressed. I thought maybe your car had been stolen. As long as you aren't stranded or anything..." Taking a chance, I turned away and took a few steps.

"My boyfriend took off and left me here," she said.

I turned back. "Do you need me to call someone for you?"

She considered this and said, "No, I've got my phone with me. I can call for a ride."

I shrugged and said, "Well, okay then." Once again, I started to leave but then made a show of being on the verge of asking something while trying not to impose.

"Hey," I stammered. "I'm heading out of here. If you need a ride somewhere, I'm not working today and I don't mind."

Her eyes narrowed in thought, then she glanced at a cheap watch strapped to her pencil wrist by a nylon wristband.

"Do you think you could give me a lift to the Mexican War Streets? I live close to there."

"No problem," I answered.

Part of me was thrilled the con had worked while part of me wanted to lecture the woman on the dangers of getting into a car with a strange man who was at least twenty years her senior. I decided to hold off on the lecture for the moment.

She offered a hand. "I'm Monica Raymund. But, Raymund with a 'u,' not an 'o.'"

"Mitch Levins," I said, drawing upon old cover ID.

We shook hands and then I pointed her toward my car. Internally, I patted myself on the back for my smooth manipulation of the girl. Sure, some of it had been good fortune. I really do like Volbeat and had seen them play in Pittsburgh. But, I'd not only managed to establish a rapport with her, but convinced her to let me drive her home. After I subtly checked the backseat for dead Lithuanian drug dealers who hated me, we got in my Volkswagen and began making our way north through the city.

"What do you do?" I asked.

Monica responded, "I work part-time for an internet marketing company in the Strip District. The rest of the time, I'm taking classes at CCAC."

I knew the Community College of Allegheny County was located only a few blocks away from the Mexican War Streets. I also knew classes were typically in-session on Wednesdays in October.

"So no work or classes today?" I asked.

"I've got an E-commerce class tonight," she replied. "I'm completing a certificate. I don't really need it, but the company I work for is paying the tuition."

I pulled the car onto the Parkway and said, "I'm sorry your boyfriend ditched you. Even if you were fighting, that's not cool."

She didn't speak and I decided not to press. A middle-aged man prying into her relationship was bound to trip a mental alarm. I was pondering other possible approaches when she spoke.

"We weren't fighting," she said while looking out the passenger-side window. "We'd gone in the theater to watch a movie, but he got all weird and jittery once we were inside. I found us some seats toward the back and we sat down. But, when the previews ended he acted all nervous and said he had to go to the bathroom. The next thing I know, he's gone and the car is gone. Now, he's not answering his phone. I'm worried about him."

"Maybe he had a family emergency," I suggested.

"Then why wouldn't he tell me? Why would he bolt like that?"

She got quiet and sniffed. Even with her head turned away from me, I could hear she was starting to cry. She pulled out her cell and I heard the clicks of typing. I couldn't see the screen, but I could guess she was texting Stretch, hoping he would respond.

"I think he might be in some kind of trouble. He tries to act all tough sometimes, but he's really a sweet, but gullible guy. In his line of work, people try to take advantage of him all the time."

"What line of work is he in?"

"He does sound recordings for lots of bands. He's even produced a few."

"Oh, yeah?" I said, sounding impressed. "Has he worked with anyone I've heard of?"

She sniffed again. "He did the latest Rat Ship record. Have you heard of them?"

I hadn't and told her so.

"He worked with Jimmy Spartan for a long time. I'm sure you've heard of him. He was more your...he was..."

"Closer to my age," I said, helping her finish the thought.

She glanced over to me with watery eyes and tried to manage a smile. Then, she looked back down to the phone in her lap and tried texting again.

"Yeah. Jimmy had been around the scene for a while," she said.

"I was always a big Jimmy Spartan fan," I said. "Your boyfriend...I'm sorry, what's his name?"

"Stretch," she said. "It's really Roger, but nobody calls him that."

"Okay. I bet Stretch really enjoyed working with Jimmy Spartan. The man was a legend."

Monica hesitated, and then said, "It was good while it

lasted. Once Jimmy died, things got weird."

"How so?" I asked while doing my best to raise my eyebrows. Which meant my expression didn't change a bit.

"I'm not sure how to explain it," she replied. "At first the cops asked him a lot of questions about Jimmy's murder. But, they left him alone after a while. I'm just afraid someone in the band got him into some other stuff. Like I said, he's kind of gullible. Gullible can be sweet, but it can also be dangerous."

"What kind of other stuff could he be involved in?" I asked.

She didn't answer.

We crossed the Fort Duquesne Bridge and exited onto the North Shore. The nighttime temperatures had been unseasonably cold for the past week and the trees in West Park were already shedding leaves like it was late November. We were almost to her neighborhood, so I was running out of time.

"It sounds like you want to help your boyfriend," I said.

She nodded enthusiastically and tried texting again. Whenever Stretch checked his phone, he'd see a chain of panicked messages from her.

I said, "Monica, I think I can help Stretch."

Her face was a mix between hope and confusion.

She started to say something, but broke off as I approached the Mexican War Streets.

Monica pointed and said, "You have to turn here."

I turned down Sherman Avenue while I talked, "The truth is I'm looking into Jimmy's murder."

Now, her expression told me she was completely dumbfounded.

"I was hired to investigate the murder specifically, but if someone has gotten Stretch involved in anything illegal, I may be able to help him. I used to be a cop. I still have plenty of friends in the department," I lied.

"So, you aren't after Stretch for something?"

"No," I said.

"Is Mitch your real name?"

"I'm Trevor Galloway. I used to work narcotics for the city."

Her mouth gaped open and she said, "Turn here."

I turned into Sampsonia Way, which was little more than a concrete path that ran between the rear entrances of row houses. Portions of the stretch were so tight, my Jetta was getting claustrophobic. I kept my eyes forward as I made the car edge along the road, and I was thinking there was barely enough room for a person to open a car door. Then right on cue, the passenger side door opened. Instinctively, I hit the brakes.

Turning to Monica I opened my mouth to speak and was greeted with a face full of pepper spray. My hands flew up to protect my face, which was not good news for my genitals. I felt a hard punch land in a soft spot and doubled over as much as one can in the front seat of a small car. I perceived a hand grasping the hair on the back of my head, and as I reached back with both my hands and to pry Monica's hand away, she slammed my now unprotected face into the steering wheel. As the pain in my nether regions grew and blood tricked down my nose, I came to the conclusion my solid rapport with Monica had degenerated.

Her hand pulled away and I raised my right arm to protect myself from any further blows while using the fingers of my left hand to try to pry open my eyelids. The pepper spray she'd hit me with was strong and she'd doused my eyes and mouth, causing me to gasp for breath. Through waves of tears, I caught snapshots of blurry images of her as my eyes refused to stay open. She stood holding the passenger side door open and I thought I caught a glimpse of a grin as she spoke.

"I told you, gullible can be dangerous, Mr. Galloway."

She slammed the car door and left me struggling to regain my vision. Trying to ignore the pain in my groin and nose, I helplessly swiveled my head and tried to process the bits and pieces of the images around me. At one point, I found myself looking over my shoulder, through the back window, and down Sampsonia Way. I thought I saw Monica's long coat flapping in the breeze. My eyes closed and I fought them open once more. Three more similar snapshots allowed me to put the frames together in my mind. The last frame was of Stretch's not-so-distressed girlfriend bounding into the passenger seat of his red Lexus. Yes, indeed. I had certainly done a masterful job of manipulating her.

A few hours later, the blood had stopped coming out of my nose. My good friend, Detective Chase Vinson had beer coming out of his.

He caught his breath, opened his mouth to say something, but started laughing again. I sat alongside him at the bar and ordered another Sam Adams.

"You..." he began. "She punched you..." he began again before tumbling into laughter. "...balls?" he managed.

My drink arrived and I continued to weather the storm.

"So, they not only made you...they got intel from you..."

Another fit of laughter, complete with a knee slap. I thought he might fall off the barstool. I was hoping he would.

"They also lured you into an alley and assaulted you."

"No," I said solemnly.

Chase calmed down.

"She assaulted me," I explained again. "Stretch was simply the getaway driver."

With that, Chase completely fell apart and was drowning in tears of amusement. I took a pull from my bottle, leaned on the bar, and rubbed my red, puffy eyes.

"You aren't helping," I muttered.

"Oh, I'm not trying," Chase chucked while raising a tall glass of Budweiser in a mock salute.

We'd been at the bar in Station Square less than thirty minutes. During that time, I'd recounted the day's adventure to Chase, skipping over my hallucinating the long-deceased Lukas Derela sitting in my car. At first, Chase had been serious and interested. Then, he was just interested. By the time I'd mentioned the words "pepper spray," he was entertained beyond belief.

He patted my back in mock sympathy. "Well, Tin Man. How do you think they made you? Did you draw attention to yourself with your happy-go-lucky personality?"

My nose wasn't broken, but it really hurt. For a skinny girl, Monica—or whatever her real name was—certainly was strong. Once I'd gotten home to clean myself up, I'd used my computer to search for the name Monica Raymund. Seeing the results felt like another punch to the privates. It turned out Monica Raymund was as actress who had starred in a television drama called *Lie to Me.* I didn't share this tidbit with Chase. I wasn't sure his heart could handle any more hysterical laughing.

"I think I know how I got made. I went back to Stretch's apartment building and took another look at the intercom system."

"And?" asked Chase expectantly.

I gritted my teeth, dreading telling him the rest. However, it was my inattention and stupidity that got me to this point in the case—which was pretty much nowhere.

"There is a small camera high on the wall above the buzzers and intercom system. The residents can see who is on the other end. Stretch spotted me outside the movie theater and devised a plan with his girlfriend. My guess is he took off and left her behind to see what level of surveillance was on him. She probably waited inside the glass doors of the theater for a few minutes and saw there weren't teams of unmarked cars chasing after Stretch. Then, she made a big show of being left behind so that even if he got rolled up, she could play the part of the innocent girlfriend."

I sipped my beer and thought of another possibility.

"Or, they weren't sure who the real target was and wanted to see who I was following. For all I know, the girlfriend has a warrant on her and she's been hiding out at Stretch's apartment. This whole thing may have been a comedy of errors on both ends," I said.

"But why take a ride with you," Chase asked. "To what end?"

I'd been giving that some thought.

"I'm not sure. On the intercom, I'd told Stretch I was looking into Jimmy's death."

I stopped in mid-drink and Chase noticed.

"What?" he asked.

"That's wrong. I told Stretch that Jimmy's family asked me to check into some things. Until I told his girlfriend what I was investigating, he may have had no idea. She was probably texting him the play-by-play while updating him with her location the entire time. Once she found out I was hired to find the killer, she...well, she did her thing."

Chase finished off his drink and said, "Well, my friend. Would you like to make an official report with the City of Pittsburgh Bureau of Police?"

"No, thank you," I said. "Your ridicule is more than enough. We don't need to expand the audience."

He chuckled and said, "I'll try and do a little more digging on Roger Orta. In the meantime, do you have any other leads?"

I told him about Jimmy Spartan's missing turntable, my trip to Planetary Electronics, and worked my way up to the attempt on my life.

"On my way back to the car, two men came up behind me," I told him. "One pulled a gun and was about to fire when Jackie shot one of the guys. They ran off. I'm sure you got a BOLO for two Eastern European types involved in a robbery."

Questions flooded Chase's face and his mouth opened, unsure which words should be the first in line. He sorted his questions, turned his hulking body toward me, and let fly.

"That was you? Jackie? *Your* Jackie? Jackie Fontree? She was one of the agents involved? What was she doing there? How did you let those guys get the drop on you? Were you armed? You do remember you're still marked, right? Derela's people haven't forgotten about you, and you let yourself get tailed? What the hell?"

I methodically worked my through his questions, neglecting to answer all the right ones. After a while, his follow up questions to my responses slowed and he became satisfied with most of my unsatisfactory answers.

Exhausted from the mix of interrogating and lecturing, Chase turned back toward the bar and rhythmically strummed his fingers on the polished mahogany surface.

"Do you think the Planetary Electronics thing will pan out?" he asked.

He saw me shrug in the mirror behind the bar.

"You said Vince Sonta is still running the business?"

"Yeah," I replied. "Along with his son, Tom."

We didn't talk for a while and Chase let his fingers generate a gentle thunder on the bar.

Finally, he said, "Hell of a coincidence that the Secret Service was on scene."

"Yep."

We looked at each other.

"Would you mind sniffing around?" I asked. "Maybe you can find out what they are working over there."

He nodded. "I'll also check in with my pawn shop contacts and see if anyone is trying to unload any old turntables."

Then, he stopped nodded and eyed me with suspicion. The suspicion shifted to worry.

"What?" I asked.

"What's wrong with you?"

I didn't even know where to start with that can of worms. In addition to dealing with my formidable personal issues, I wasn't exactly feeling terrific about watching my client commit suicide, jeopardizing Jackie's investigation, getting blown-off by Roger Orta, and ultimately getting my ass kicked by a Miley Cyrus lookalike. I'd had better weeks. I'd had worse.

"I'm fine," I answered.

"That's what I mean," said Chase. "You seem awfully mellow about all of this."

A bit defensively, I said, "How should I be acting?"

"Like you," he said.

"Meaning?"

He considered this for a moment.

"Angry. In fact, you should be furious."

"I'm not happy about all of this," I said in an even tone. "I don't like it when people try to kill me."

He shook his head. "This is different than before. You're missing...rage. As long as I've known you, no matter how calm you seemed to be on the surface, people could always sense rage in you. You're like a cheap cigarette lighter."

"Very flattering," I said.

He ignored me and kept talking. "People spin that metal

wheel and sparks flicker, but the flame doesn't always catch. But, after a few times..."

Chase made a whooshing sound that I understood to be a flame.

"People see it behind your eyes," he continued. "They feel it radiating from you. Some people try to ignore it, but they know it's there. Or, at least it was."

"Maybe I'm out of fluid," I suggested.

"That's not good," he opined. "Your anger drove you. It kept you alive when things were at their worst. Fierceness can be a positive thing, and I'm not getting that vibe from you right now."

"I've been working on controlling my temper," I said. "I'm getting too old to be angry."

The concern clung to my friend's face.

He said, "You've lost a lot over the years. Most of it was taken from you. Nevertheless, it's lost. Are you sure you want to lose the one constant in your arsenal? A compass that's been singed by flames is better than none at all."

I reassured Chase that I would be fine.

It would all be fine.

Just fine.

I told him I'd call him in a day or two, retrieved my jacket from a neighboring bar stool, and walked out to my car. I'd left the windows rolled down, but the interior still smelled like pepper spray. I let the car idle and tried to let me eyes blur through the windshield. I let everything go out of focus and waited for my mind to take over, guide me to a lead; a revelation; a hunch. Breathing deeply, I invited the blur-out. I beckoned it to take me to the crime scene. Then, I begged it to take me anywhere.

To show me anything.

I saw nothing.

My eyes refocused as beads of water fell on the windshield. What now constituted a harmless autumn shower would wreak chaos on the roadways in a few weeks, when the droplets would turn to ice. The drops piled up until they joined together, became heavy, and streaked down the windshield. I activated the wipers, flung them away, and threw the car into drive. I'd go get some sleep for now, but compass or no compass, I had to keep moving.

The knocking seemed like a dream. In fact, I was fairly sure it was a dream. I awoke disoriented and less than sober thanks to the additional beers I'd had upon arriving home. I'd drifted off in bed with a paperback in one hand and a bottle in the other. The clock blazed 12:15 a.m. and I convinced myself I'd been stirred by a fitful dream that had evaporated as quickly as it had formed.

Through the rain tapping on my bedroom window, I heard it again. Like the rain, the knocking wasn't urgent, but tentative and steady. Rubbing my eyes, I put myself together the best I could, grabbed my gun, and walked to the door.

"Yes," I said.

"It's me."

"Hold on."

I tucked the gun into a desk drawer and started to unlock the door. Suddenly, I realized I must look like hell and smell like stale beer. A minute later I'd splashed water in my face and used mouthwash in a feeble effort to make myself presentable.

I opened the door, cleared my throat and said, "Hi."

I stood aside and Jackie accepted the silent invitation.

"I guess I woke you," she said.

"It's okay," I said, closing the door behind her. I took her coat and tossed it onto a chair.

She inventoried her surroundings the same way she'd done before. Her eyes slid from one corner to another, then to the walls, then to me. I studied her face and saw things I'd rarely seen in her. She had her walls down. A mix of apprehension, vulnerability, and caring were present and I didn't sense resentment or mistrust in her eyes. She was here today, not yesterday, and not years ago. Today. The bad things I'd done weren't shadowing her at this exact moment in time. She stood there, her hair damp from the rain, watching me watch her.

"This doesn't mean anything," she said. "I'm not saying it means nothing, but it doesn't necessarily mean anything."

I took what felt like the first breath I'd taken in minutes. "Okay," I said.

"Just don't apologize, or justify, or explain," she said. Her eyes were wet and everything about her seemed soft.

"Just be here," she said.

My heart ached for her. My arms longed for her.

"I am," I told her.

I didn't dare move. Finally, she did and moved over to me. She put her hands on my face and stroked my cheeks.

"I still hate you," she said.

"Me too," I said.

She put her lips on mine and we kissed. The longer we kissed, the more we let the dark parts of our history take backstage to the better days. As we made love, my failures became more dream-like. More unreal. They became like hallucinations that would haunt and hurt, but perhaps could drift into the background of a new reality.

This doesn't mean anything, she'd said.

It didn't mean nothing. I knew that with all my heart. Even a single night of absolution means something to the damned.

* * *

She was propped up on one elbow and staring at me when I woke. I stared at her with a combination of relief and dread. I was relieved she was here and was real. I was dreading hearing what she would say. Before I'd been able to turn my body in her direction, my mind was already hearing her talk about how her coming here had been a mistake. I imagined her coming to her senses and reminding me how I'd pushed her away and betrayed her trust. In a terrifying flash, I saw her walking out the door, never to return. I swallowed hard and waited.

Her lips hinted at a smile and I felt the gesture through my entire being.

"Oh...my...God," she said. Her face lit up with disbelief.

Quickly, I leaned up on an elbow. "What?"

"You just smiled. The Tin Man smiled," she said, her face lighting up.

I stared at her dumfounded. "I did?"

"You did," she said proudly.

Something coiled around my heart relaxed as I watched her laugh at me. She didn't have one foot out the door. She wasn't sulking, regretting, or fretting. She was still in my bed and this was happening. In fact, it was the most real thing I'd experienced in a long time.

I tried to speak, but had difficulty forming any words. With her lying naked beside me, I felt I was on the surface of a bubble and the slightest disturbance would cause all of this to go away and allow us to sink into nothingness. She noticed me struggling and tilted her head with kindness and compassion.

"You don't have to say all the right words," she told me.

"I'm not worried about that," I said. "But, I don't want to say the wrong ones."

She smiled again and slid the sheets down her body. "Let's play it safe and not use any words right this minute."

Later, we drank coffee at my kitchen table and tiptoed through conversation. Our small talk gradually grew large enough to cast a shadow, as is often the case when the road behind you has more than its share of rough patches. However, things remained pleasant enough between the two of us, even when the discussion turned serious.

"You were a little tipsy when I got here last night."

"I was," I agreed.

"Is that normal for you?"

"No," I said truthfully. "I was out with Chase and then had a few too many when I got home. I've had a lot on my mind."

"Such as?"

"You."

She smiled again and said, "You know, they say it's not good to drink alone."

I decided if I assured her that with my mind I was never truly alone, it would do little to comfort her.

Rather than respond, I did nothing but watch her smile. Somehow, Jackie's smile was more hypnotic than Dr. Welch's. Her way of moving was more seductive. I drank my coffee and wondered what my psychiatrist would say about this new development.

"Is that all?" asked Jackie. "I'd hate to think that seeing me again drove you to drink."

"Not just you," I admitted. "I ran into some trouble with the case I'm working."

"Want to tell me about it?"

Being fully aware I'm not exactly an open book, I decided to fight every instinct I had to be quiet. I set my mug on the table, leaned forward, and laid out the Jimmy Spartan case. Which, I had to admit, wasn't as much of a case as it was a debacle as far as my involvement was concerned. Jackie listened intently, perked up when I explained the real reason for my trip to visit Vince Sonta at Planetary Electronics, and then politely bit her lip as I told her about my being pummeled by the girl calling herself Monica Raymund.

"You used to be able to fight," she said. "I still remember that amateur boxer coming at you when we were serving a warrant on him. You took him apart in short-order. What happened to you?"

"I got caught off-guard," I said.

"I'd say so," she said. Her smile faded and she added, "You can't get complacent, Trevor."

"I know."

She finished her coffee and stood. My stomach tightened as the moment approached when she would leave. She would leave and perhaps never come back. I knew that once Jackie was out of my sight and able to objectively dive into her own mind, her being with me would make less and less sense. I'd be nothing more than a new egregious error piled on top of a previous mistake. Scar tissue above scar tissue. In due time, she'd regain her sanity and leave my life again. My skin felt cold. My heart raced. My head began to hurt. She was a drug that had been injected back into my life and I was already bracing for the withdrawal. Once an addict, always an addict.

I exhaled when she refilled her mug and returned to the table.

"Are you okay? You look pale."

I nodded. "Do you have to go to work today?"

"Administrative suspension," she answered without any animosity toward me.

"Do they know how long?"

Under one of my dress shirts, she shrugged a shoulder. "A few days, I guess."

"Okay," I said, because "Good" wouldn't have sounded quite right and too many apologies make the act meaningless.

"Trevor, I don't want to start an argument, but did you notice anything odd going on at Planetary Electronics?"

I shook my head and said, "So you were in fact staking it out? That's why you asked me if I was into something illegal. You've been watching Vince and thought I might be wrapped up in something."

She sipped and thought, weighing how much she could tell me. With two fingers she gently guided some strands of her hair away from her face.

"Two months ago, Cranberry Township PD responded to a traffic accident on Route 19," she began. I was familiar with the Pittsburgh suburb situated north of the city. It wasn't the type of place most crime stories started. It was the type of place boring golf stories originated.

Jackie continued. "A white Cadillac Escalade heading south on 19 crossed Route 228 and was T-boned by a soccer mom trying to beat a red light."

"Okay," I said.

"The cops found the driver of the Escalade unconscious and the paramedics took him to ER. But, while the officers were checking the car to see if there were any other passengers who had bounced around in the back, they noticed cash spilled out all over the place. Some sort of container in the back of the SUV had broken during the crash and the money had scattered throughout the passenger compartment."

"How much money?" I asked.

"Two hundred thousand," she said.

I tried to let out an admiring whistle. It was weak.

She went to take a drink of her coffee, but spilled it down the front of her white shirt—my white shirt—because she was laughing at me. "You never could whistle worth a damn. But, I agree with the sentiment. Do you still keep laundry stain remover above your washing machine?"

I stuttered dumbly, and it became obvious I had no idea that I'd ever had laundry stain remover anywhere in the house.

"Never mind, I'll go look," she said while smiling and shaking her head. "If you don't mind, pour me another coffee and I'll finish the story when I get back."

I used a dishtowel to mop up the spillage on the table and then poured coffee into Jackie's mug.

Jackie's mug.

I sure liked the sound of that.

I was drifting back and forth between memories and fantasies in which Jackie and I shared trivial possessions that no longer seemed trivial, when there was a knock at the front door.

Not wanting to seem paranoid, I didn't go to the bedroom where Jackie was changing in order to get my gun. Not wanting to get chastised for being complacent, I pulled a long blade from the knife block sitting on the counter and then walked toward the front door. I stood back several feet and off to the side before speaking.

"Who is it?" I asked.

The door exploded inward and the frame splintered as if it was made of truck-stop toothpicks. I had just enough time to put myself into a defensive stance with the knife at the ready, when a compact man with sharp Hispanic features walked through the threshold and leveled a Glock at me. I wasn't entirely sure of his intent until the moment he shot me in the head. The last thing that went through my head, other than a bullet, was the thought that I needed to warn Jackie. I opened my mouth to yell, but never managed to make a sound.

TRACK 7
"LIKE A HOLE IN THE HEAD"

I'd been cut. I'd been beaten. I'd been filled to the brim with narcotics. But, I'd never been shot. It turns out it's tremendously painful. Of course, I didn't actually remember any sensations from the exact moment the bullet struck my skull and skidded along the right side of my head. However once the pain meds wore off in the hospital, the newly created trench burned and ached. Later, I learned I had Jackie to thank for some of the discomfort since she had told both the responding EMTs and the doctors at the hospital that I was a recovering addict and avoided taking anything stronger than a Tylenol.

When I had begun to regain consciousness five hours after the shooting, I heard Jackie's voice emanating from somewhere close. I blinked hard, which hurt. I stopped blinking, which also hurt. As my eyes focused, I found Jackie sitting beside my bed, which was covered with sheets that were more eggshell than white.

"You're at Mercy," she said, knowing I'd understand she was referring to the name of the hospital.

I nodded, or thought I did.

"You've been shot in the head, but you're going to be fine. The bullet hit your Tin Man skull and somehow didn't penetrate far. You've got stitches and possibly a concussion from hitting your head on the floor."

I made a poor attempt at speaking, cleared my throat and tried again.

"Were you hurt?" I rasped.

She shook her head. "I ran out of the bedroom, saw you on the floor, and heard a car speeding away. I'm so sorry, Trevor. I should have gotten out there sooner."

"No," I said. "He would have shot you too."

She grasped my hand tight. "Did you see who shot you?"

"A male. He was about five-eight, one hundred eighty pounds, possible Hispanic decent, black hair, wearing jeans, a black fleece pullover, and he shot me with a Glock."

"Had you ever seen him before?" she asked.

I told her I hadn't. Then I reached up and let my fingers find the bandage stretched around my head.

"They had to shave that side of your head and put in some stitches," Jackie said. "You are going to look silly for a while."

Honestly, that was the least of my concerns. In a few days, I'd shave off the rest of my hair, plop a Pirates cap on top, and go about my business. The problem was *my business* inexplicably involved getting attacked by people I didn't know. I needed a new business model and I needed it fast.

"When can I get out of here?" I asked.

Jackie was dumbfounded.

She squeezed my hand a little harder, but not with affection. "You were shot in the head. You are not going anywhere until the doctors give you a clean bill of health. If they say you need to be here for a month, then you will be here for a month. This is not up for debate."

I knew not to argue because she wasn't using contractions. You never argued with Jackie when she didn't use contractions. Ever.

A nurse entered the room, checked my vitals, and offered me to get me a couple of Tylenol that would undoubtedly show up on my insurance statement as costing two hundred dollars. I declined the pills and she shot me a sideways glance that said, *I know you're acting tough in front of your girlfriend. I'll ask you again later.* The nurse then politely informed Jackie that visiting hours were over and told her I needed my rest.

"Before you go," I said after the nurse bowed out of the room. "Finish the story you were telling me."

She squinted and tilted her head.

"The one about the car crash and the money in the SUV."

She put up a hand and said, "Not another word about that right now. We will talk tomorrow. Get some sleep and I will be back first thing in the morning."

She kissed me on the cheek and once on my bandaged head. Then, she left the room. I drifted off hoping that when she returned, she did so with some answers. And maybe some contractions.

Some people speak regretfully of being unable to remember dreams. I sometimes wonder if those people would feel the same way if they really could remember their nighttime fantasies. Would they really wake in the morning and smile about lighthearted encounters and pleasurable adventures? Or would they remember dreams like mine, where shadows spread out from the corners to consume anything one might consider good or reassuring? I remember my dreams. I remember what I dreamt in the hospital.

I was standing downtown at the intersection of Ross Street and Fifth Avenue. It was night and not a soul stirred on the streets. No cars, buses, or homeless drifters patrolling their beats and searching for hope. I looked up and couldn't see any stars in spite of the black canvas being cloudless. There was nothing but the constant low hum of streetlights that somehow seemed to create an ominous harmony. I was wearing a suit—something I haven't done in years. My head dropped and I noticed a red tie draped perfectly flat down my white shirt. With one hand, I lifted the tie and rubbed the slick material between my fingers. I let go of the tie and it fell to its original position with a wet smack. Touching the tie again, I found it was now soaked and heavy with some sort of liquid.

My gaze fell below the tie and down to my feet. My black shoes shined to the point I could see the one of the surrounding traffic lights reflected on their surface. The green reflection switched to yellow and the streetlight hum was interrupted by the mechanical clicking noises of the traffic signal beginning cycling through yellow to red. The clicking sequence restarted as a light on the opposite corner ran its cycle. Then the other two followed in quick succession and I found myself standing in the intersection, illuminated by the surrounding red bulbs.

Turning as slow as the shadow cast by a sundial, I pivoted to look down Ross Street. On the right side of the street was the Allegheny County Courthouse. On the left side sat what many believe to be an architectural masterpiece, the Old Allegheny County Jail. Over Ross Street, spanning the space between the courthouse and former jail, was the Bridge of Sighs, copied from Venice's more famous bridge bearing that name. But, this wasn't Italy. It was Pittsburgh and I knew Pittsburgh. And I knew something was wrong with that bridge.

Taking a step forward, I saw all the traffic signals simultaneously switch to green. The transition was announced by the same click I had heard before, but now the clicking persisted although the lights did not change color. I kept moving toward the bridge and tried to discern what was wrong with the arched design. The clicking became rhythmic and echoed off the building's sand-colored bricks that conveyed the permanence of justice. I squinted as the volume increased and stopped walking when it seemed the sound was no longer everywhere, but right beside me. I turned to my right and saw a clock mounted on the wall of the courthouse. It was the same clock that ticked during my sessions with Dr. Welch. It contained the same second hand that to me promised false certainty.

I stared at the clock and became conscious of the fact I wasn't breathing. Forcing myself to continue on my way, I turned and took more slow strides toward the bridge. My throat felt tight and I pulled at the collar of my shirt as I began to see what had been bothering me about the elevated pathway that had been walked by countless prisoners who learned their fate not long after crossing into the courthouse.

Two prongs hung down from the far side of the bridge that normally had a smooth underside. Shadows crept in from each corner of the bridge and began to obscure the path I had taken to get to the bridge. Now, nothing was in the light other than me and the bridge. Moving under the bridge, I cleared my throat, struggling to take in air. Attempting to loosen my wet tie, I walked completely through the arch and gazed up to see what seemed to be hanging from the far side of the structure.

It was a man. One end of a rope was tied around his neck and the other end must have been attached to something inside the narrow window at the bridge's midpoint. From the intersection, I had been seeing his feet dangling just below the arch. I pulled again at my tie, which seemed to be tightening and stared up at the man who was staring back at me. He blinked. My tie constricted. He blinked.

Oxygen seeped through my throat. He blinked. My air stopped. My lungs burned. I fought to dig my fingers under my collar, but there was no space to find. A scratchy laugh came from above as I dropped to my knees and the shadows drew closer. Somehow, I found the strength to raise my head to take one last look at the man on the bridge.

From above, Jimmy Spartan smiled the smile that had helped make him a star and said, "It all starts with a mistake, Mr. Galloway."

The darkness consumed us both.

"Well, you're a dead man."

"News to me," I said, rubbing my eyes.

Chase closed the door behind him and took a swig from a Starbucks cup. He grinned as he scooted a chair next to the hospital bed. His muscular mass molded around the rickety wooden chair and I wondered if it might not collapse under his weight.

"Why are you so chipper?" I asked.

"I told you. You're deceased."

I massaged the back of my neck as I looked around the room and then at the heavily tattooed mammoth who was informing me of my unfortunate fate.

"So, this is Hell," I surmised.

Chase leaned in and patted my arm with the hand not holding the cup. I sniffed the air.

"What in the world are you drinking?"

His smile dissipated and he stammered, "A caramel brulée latte."

I assessed him to see if he was kidding. In all the years I'd known Chase, I'd never seen him drink anything than black coffee, domestic beer, straight whiskey, iced tea, or water if none of the aforementioned choices were available.

Other than him owning a six-year-old Chihuahua named Cujo, the man's personality, food choices, apartment, and overall demeanor matched perfectly with his appearance.

After a lengthy silence, he shrugged a broad deltoid muscle, raised the cup, and said, "What? It's tasty."

I stopped rubbing my neck and found a button that adjusted my bed so I was closer to vertical than horizontal.

I said, "You mentioned something about my death."

"For all intents and purposes, you are a homicide statistic," Chase said proudly. "It took some politicking on my end, but the official story coming from the department is that an unnamed man was shot in killed at your address last night." He sipped his candy-in-a-cup and said, "My condolences."

"You could have asked me first," I said sharply. "I could have notified a few people who might be worried about me."

Chase eased back and his chair moaned. "Exactly who would you have had me notify?"

He had me there. The only people I cared about who would hear the news were Jackie and Chase.

Dodging his question, I asked, "Who from the department is coming to interview me?"

"Paul Kent and Steve Willis."

"Solid?" I asked.

"They're solid," said Chase. "Any history with you?"

"No," I replied. "Never heard of them."

We sat for a minute, not articulating that it was a good thing I didn't have history with the detectives since, in my case, having a history with someone was usually a bad thing. When I'd been debriefed after my abduction, I couldn't even provide my inquisitors with a list of all the names, operations, and informants I'd given over to my captors. I remembered quick flashes that blended into drug-induced hallucinations accompanied by excruciating pain.

For all I knew, I'd compromised every narcotics operation in the department and half those detectives could have moved on to other squads like Missing Persons or possibly Burglary. The fact Kent and Willis would know me by reputation only, might make things go smoother. Suddenly, it occurred to me that the interview was several hours overdue.

"Why weren't they here yesterday when I first woke up?"

Chase beamed. "Oh, they tried. Believe me, they tried."

For a moment, I was confused as to what could have possibly prevented two detectives, who were accustomed to going toe-to-toe with the worst the city had to offer, from coming into my room. Then, I knew.

"Jackie," I said.

"Jackie," Chase said with a chuckle. "She whipped out her federal credentials the moment she saw them coming down the hall."

"This isn't a Hollywood production. I'm sure Kent and Willis ignored that move."

Chase laughed. "Oh, they did. Which pissed her off royally. She let into them like there was no tomorrow, said she'd already gotten the suspect's description from you and that she had been in the house at the time of the shooting. She told them that you were fighting for your life and couldn't be disturbed. From the way Kent and Willis tell it, she was determined to shoot anyone right then and there who might bother you."

"She always was protective," I said.

Even as the words slid from my mouth, something seemed off. Jackie could be prone to over-reaction, and God knew she had a temper, but my gut was telling me her protectiveness had more than one purpose.

That train of thought ran afoul of the tracks when Chase said, "So, now that you're no longer among the living, and presumably safe from whoever tried to kill you, what is on your agenda?"

I pushed a button and let my bed recline.

"Jackie is coming by soon and we are going to talk about two things: cars and money."

"Where did I leave off?"

"A wreck on Route 19. White Cadillac Escalade, injured driver and two hundred thousand in cash," I reminded Jackie.

Her hair was down today. It always looked best that way. She sat at the foot of the bed, with one leg up and the other dangling toward the floor. She was absolutely radiant against the backdrop of the drab pistachio wall.

"Right," she said. "So, the responding officers find this cash and all of it is in hundreds. Naturally, they become extremely inquisitive, but nobody can question the driver because he's at the hospital and nobody knows if he's ever going to regain consciousness. The township detective responds to the scene and examines the money. Now, this detective—Linda Caguno—she's attended some of the seminars the Secret Service holds and knows how to distinguish genuine currency from counterfeit notes."

"Notes?" I asked.

She shook her head derisively and smirked. "I guess you should have attended our seminars too. We call them notes. As in Federal Reserve Notes. That's the official name for currency."

"Not money?" I said.

"Money and currency are general terms, aren't they? They are everything from the value attached to your credit card purposes to the electronic ones and zeros that transfer via computer every time there is a wire transfer. Even the pennies in your pocket fall into those categories."

I pulled my sheets down to display my hospital gown

that was somehow an uglier shade of green than the walls.

"I don't have any pockets. My ass isn't even covered."

Amazingly, she was able to ignore my wit and continue with the explanation.

"But when someone refers to Federal Reserve Notes, it's understood we are talking about U.S. paper currency."

Pulling the sheets back up so I could spare others from having to see my gown, I said, "What did Detective Caguno find?"

"The notes appeared to be real. They were the old 1996 series which are still in circulation. The worn paper felt legitimate, the security strip was in place, the color-shifting ink was there...it all looked good."

"Since you are telling me this story, I'm guessing this doesn't end up being some funny story where the driver was part of some big misunderstanding," I said.

Jackie smiled. "No. As Caguno went through the notes, she discovered some of the serial numbers were repeated."

"That's not supposed to happen," I said.

"It certainly is not, and she knew it. Caguno called our office and we ran the serial numbers through our system. They were flagged in our database as having been previously logged as fake bills."

"Notes," I helpfully corrected.

She punched me in the leg and said, "Right." Her playful flame reduced to a flicker and she said, "This stuff is good, Trevor. We've been chasing these notes all over the world and we're hardly making a dent. The product is so good, even those who have an eye for counterfeit assume the notes are genuine."

Although counterfeiting wasn't in my wheelhouse, I had read a number of stories about it over the years. You don't work in narcotics and not come across people trying to pass bad paper for drugs. But, the quality Jackie was talking

about was light years beyond junkies using cheap laser print-
ers to crank out flimsy reproductions on basic copier paper.
What she was talking about was high-scale. What she was
talking about was organized. I searched my memory for the
articles I had read and one word came to mind.

"Colombia?" I said.

Years ago, Colombia had become a major player in financial crimes, specifically counterfeiting. The notes origi-
nating from the drug capital of the world had flaws, but
would pass detection unless closely examined.

Jackie stood and stretched. "Not anymore. Now it's
Peru."

"Peru? Why Peru?"

She shivered and walked over to the thermostat. I watched
her push buttons until we heard heat push through the vents.

Jackie explained, "The Colombian government finally
cracked down on counterfeiting. However, the outfits simply
relocated to Peru and that's when things got interesting.
The enterprise is under the control of organized crime syn-
dicates who have dedicated time and resources to improv-
ing the process of counterfeiting. They are using giant off-
set printing presses, well-made plates with the currency
design, thick bond paper, and are simulating most security
features."

I sat up as much as the bed would allow me. "What
about the security thread that is actually in the paper? Isn't
that usually a game changer?"

"Inserting it by hand," she said.

I was confused. "How is that possibly efficient? Are you
telling me they have a workforce dedicated to sitting at
tables to insert security threads into notes one at a time?"

"That's exactly what I'm saying."

I thought about the implications of what I had learned.
If what Jackie was saying was true, which I knew it had to

be, then organized networks were hiring or forcing scores of people to perform precision work for an enterprise that had a direct effect on the U.S. economy. I feared that if the product was good enough to fool the public then it might be good enough to fool the real gatekeepers. It could fool the banks.

"How close to perfect are we talking about with the Peruvian notes?"

"It's some of the best we've ever seen, but it still has flaws. They don't have our paper, which is actually a linen-cotton mix that won't disintegrate when exposed to water. Financial institutions pick them out quickly because there are some other issues with the microprinting in the lower left portion of on the front of the one hundred dollar notes. There are also some other indicators we don't disclose to the public."

So, the counterfeit was passable when circulated among consumers and business, but not banks or the Federal Reserve. I assumed that meant the street value couldn't be astronomical and I said as much to Jackie.

"It's still running at twenty to twenty-five cents on the dollar," she said.

That meant that the two hundred thousand discovered in the crash north of the city wasn't chump change. That driver had lost counterfeit notes with a street value of nearly fifty thousand dollars. My narcotics detective mind went to work and I started to see how this played out.

"The driver lived, and rolled. He's had to become your informant because he was facing federal charges and had become a liability to people involved in Peruvian organized crime."

She sat on the end of the bed. "Close. His name was Lloyd Ellwood. We covered up his involvement in the accident and his arrest for distribution of counterfeit currency.

Over a two-week period, during which he never left the hospital, he gave us enough information to prove he was valuable. We were working on officially registering him as a C.I. when he unexpectedly died from an aneurism."

The world of narcotics wasn't greatly different than many other criminal operations, so I knew two things. First, Ellwood wasn't a Peruvian name and organized crime networks typically keep their inner-circles homogenous when it comes to race and ethnicity. Therefore, Ellwood was likely a low to mid-level courier at best. Second, given Ellwood would have limited access to, or information about, the inner-workings of an international crime syndicate, the Secret Service was hoping to use him to work up the chain, which was likely to discover the point and method of importation. For Ellwood to prove he had any value, he had to have given up at least one name or one location.

Jackie was describing how Ellwood's aneurism had ruptured and how the medical staff had rushed him off to surgery. She was saying something about the man hanging on and how his fate was uncertain for the first couple of hours, but her voice soon faded from my ears. The greens and whites in the room became indistinguishable from each other and objects in my proximity blurred into the chasm. My focus was nowhere and everywhere. My mind pulled in facts and filled in the blanks with detailed logical fictions. The room transformed to the intersection of Routes 19 and 228 in Cranberry Township.

I watched as steam poured out of the front of the crumpled Escalade and I breathed in the smell of antifreeze and burned rubber. A trickle of horns blasted at the busy intersection, but those noises came from drivers whose cars were far back from the intersection and could not see the obvious reason their line of traffic was not moving forward. I could see vaguest outline of a man with his head leaning back in the driver's seat of the white SUV. On the over side of the Escalade was a minivan, the airbag deployed. I was on the west side of the intersection, but I saw a man who had been heading east on 228 jump down from a dump truck. He was talking into a cell phone as he approached the scene. The world spun for me and suddenly I was on the other side of the two cars and beside the man on the phone. He spoke in short sentences and for some reason I couldn't make out the words although I knew he was giving a dispatcher the location.

My world shifted again and I was behind the Escalade. I felt some time has passed. The driver of the dump truck was gone and police cars were arriving from everywhere. EMTs had opened the doors of both the Escalade and the minivan and I walked to a point where I had an angle to see through the Escalade's driver's side window. Ellwood was there, but was not responding to the medics. The soccer mom was still behind the wheel of the minivan and another EMT was putting her in a neck brace as she sobbed. An officer, who looked like he might have been old enough to legally drink, walked past me while he chewed gum. He was working the gum aggressively in an effort to appear calm. Like he'd seen all this before. He wasn't a rookie. He'd been there.

I've been there kid. Chew that gum. Pray to God you always hold on to some minor subconscious act, like chewing gum, that hides your insecurities as long as possible. Someday you won't need to chew gum, use black humor, or have that stiff drink at the end of your shift, and that's when you'll have to ask yourself if you've seen too much.

I followed the kid to the back of the Escalade and he reached a hand out to open the back, but paused. He was unsure and looked around for a supervisor or more experienced officer. But, they'd just arrived. Some were positioning their cars to block traffic while others were rapidly deploying flares that magically explode into amber and smell of heavy sulfur.

The young officer's fingers found the handle that should open the rear hatch of the SUV and he pressed something until he heard a pop. He wondered who he might find. This wasn't the academy and it wasn't a movie. The blood would be real and any disfigurement he would witness would reflect its grotesqueness in his memories forever.

It's okay, kid. Open it up. I knew it was safe and there was nothing horrid to see. I knew this, not just because Jackie had told me nobody else had been in the vehicle, but because now I knew exactly what was in the back. At my table, before I had been shot, Jackie had said that a container in the back of the SUV had broken and the assumption was that container was where the money had been hidden. It wasn't simply a *container.*

The Secret Service stakeout.

The counterfeit money—smuggled into the country.

The courier.

The need to find the point of import.

How could one sneak counterfeit money into the country?

Who did I know who had foreign contacts regularly sending items to the U.S.?

The officer tugged on the door and the hatch lifted. There it was, partially covered by one hundred dollar bills. One side had cracked during the impact which had let the top portion slide off enough to allow the counterfeit to flow from the shell. The officer's face was one of puzzlement. I knew what he was thinking. If I were in his shoes, I would have been thinking the exact same thing.

Why in the hell would anyone stuff money into an old record player?

Jackie touched my leg and the scene in my mind waved

and distorted as if a stone had been thrown into the pond of my consciousness. The ripples subsided and the room came back into focus. Jackie was still talking about the life-saving efforts performed on Lloyd Ellwood. She was halfway through a sentence when I interrupted her.

"The counterfeit was in a record player or turntable, wasn't it?"

Jackie shifted slightly and seemed surprised. "Yes."

"Have you confirmed Vince Sonta is involved?" I asked.

She shook her head. "Ellwood gave up Planetary Electronics as a distribution center. He wouldn't give up any names until an agreement was in place. Then, he was going to work for us, pick up a shipment, and help us roll up his contacts who we hoped would help us identify the source in Peru."

"It's Vince," I said sadly. "I think it's just him and his son Tom running the place. Vince is the one who knows collectors all over the world."

Jackie shrugged. "It seems logical, although there are some other employees. As of late, Vince and Tom seem to run a small crew that work a few hours for them and spend the rest of their time in the part of the shop where they sell records. They're all about Tom's age and seem to be tight with each other. We tailed each member of the crew and identified most of them through their license plates or hotel registrations. Two of them show up in NCIC as having petty criminal histories and the other two are clean."

I thought about seeing Vince and Tom at the store and started to wonder if I had spooked them to the point they would do something desperate.

I asked, "Do any of the crew match the description of the man who shot me?"

Jackie shook her head. "That was one of the first things I considered. Three of the guys are white and one is of

Moroccan descent."

I have many shortcomings, but I've always had a talent for identifying nationalities, or at least general ethnic types. There was no chance I had mistaken the shooter's features as Hispanic rather than Moroccan.

"The shooter could have been Peruvian," I said.

"I know," said Jackie. "But you talked to Vince Sonta about the Jimmy Spartan case and never gave him any reason to think you were interested in counterfeiting. It would be insane for Peruvian organized crime to send a hitter after you unless they had substantial reasons to believe you were a threat."

She was right. All I had asked about was one antique turntable that had belonged to an aging rock star. Counterfeiting wasn't even on my radar. For a criminal organization to risk exposure there had to be a strong motive such as protecting an ongoing illicit enterprise. Or, in the case of my Eastern European drug gang friends, a psychotic need for revenge. While my old enemies were a closed loop of sadists, I couldn't discount the possibility the organization had put some sort of open contract on me. Maybe the group's leadership had decided having a direct hand in my death wasn't as important as shielding themselves from scrutiny. Or, maybe someone was attempting to impress the group in order to gain acceptance from a group that typically included only those from Lithuania, Estonia, and other former Soviet republics.

Maybe.

Maybe.

Maybe.

Maybe is an uncomfortable place to be when someone thinks your life is worth nothing. *Maybe* is an uncomfortable place to be when dangerous men believe the taking of your life means everything. *Certainty* can mean Heaven or it can mean Hell, but *maybe* is purgatory. There is something inspiring in the famous quote: "If you are going through Hell, keep going." But when you are hanging in that space in-between paradise and damnation, it's not that simple. You can thrust forward to battle your way out of the vines and thickets. But, can you be sure which fate you will find at the end of your charge? Will purgatory seem better or worse in comparison?

"The way I see it," Jackie began, "Either one of your old enemies came calling, or the shooter is related to the Jimmy Spartan case. It's unlikely you being shot had anything to do with the Secret Service's investigation."

Her viewpoint was logical and I told her so.

"What have you learned from your surveillance?" I asked.

Jackie sighed. "Not as much as we would have liked. As I told you, we've identified the possible players and run their histories. From the surveillance van, we've been able to watch some of the incoming and outgoing deliveries and followed a few to their final destinations. We're hoping we find someone who gets frequent deliveries from Planetary Electronics because, while I'm sure Vince has his repeat customers, it's not the type of business that would demand regular trips to the same customers."

That made sense, and the Secret Service really had no other options considering the small amount of information that had been provided by Lloyd Ellwood. Even if the agency suspected a delivery to Planetary Electronics contained a record player filled with counterfeit currency, they would have trouble getting a warrant to search the package. Even then, they wouldn't want to seize the package, but would want to track it to its destination. Following the package would involve planting a tracker in the record player which would be easily discovered if an expert like Vince Sonta inspected the machinery inside.

Jackie and her fellow agents were doing things the right way. They would find out who received monthly or bi-monthly deliveries from Vince, follow that person to a courier, and tail the courier to the distributor. The agents would try to observe a deal for the fake money and trail behind the buyer. Once the buyer spent any of the counterfeit notes, the agents would arrest him and start working back up the chain. Since the agent would already know the players, they would put the buyer in an interrogation room and lay it all out for him so he could see his only choice was to testify against the courier. The courier would testify against the distributor. The distributor would roll on Vince and Vince would have to roll on his Peruvian connection. And so goes the game of human dominos.

"You should probably take another look at what you've done on the Spartan case," Jackie advised. "It's possible that somewhere along the line, you stumbled upon a snake pit."

She was right. It was the most reasonable explanation. Not only did I need to get back to working the case, but I needed to do a much better job than I had thus far. If I was going to get killed over a cold case, then I wanted to at least be killed because I intentionally got closer to the truth. So far, I had been stumbling around and embarrassing myself. Fortunately, only a few people knew about my bumbling and I hoped it would stay that way. News of incompetence has a way of spreading like wildfire, but I was hoping for the best.

I started to say something to Jackie when two men walked into the room. The taller of the detectives had caramel skin and the long arms that extended down his thin frame could have been made from copper wire. He was in his fifties and seemed to be the tofu and coconut water type. The other man was maybe thirty-five and smelled of old cigarettes. His yellowish face was partially obscured by a goatee that did not suit him. Both men looked sheepishly at Jackie until she gave them an approving nod. Once they felt reassured Jackie wouldn't impale them for disturbing me, the smoker was the first to pull out a badge and speak.

"Mr. Galloway, I'm Detective Willis. This is Detective Kent. We're here to talk to you about what happened."

"If that's okay?" said Kent, but he wasn't looking at me. He was still keeping an eye on Jackie to see if her tail rattled.

"It's fine," I said. "Please come in."

Jackie looked around the room and seeing only the one chair she and Chase had been using during their visits, said, "I'll go see if I can find another chair and then I'll leave you guys alone to talk."

Maybe it was just me, but the detectives appeared relieved to hear that last part.

Jackie walked out and Willis pulled out a notepad.

"How are you feeling?" he asked.

"Not bad considering I was shot in the head," I answered.

"What about your other wounds?" Kent asked.

"What other wounds?"

The detectives paused for effect and glanced at each other before turning back to me. Willis said, "Our mistake, I guess. We'd heard reports that you'd had your ass kicked by some girl who was taking a break from watching the Disney Channel."

Kent was the first of the two to smile. Then they both laughed good-naturedly. It sucked.

News of incompetence. It spreads like wildfire.

TRACK 8
"FOOLED ME TWICE (THE HEART OF SHAME)"

The questioning by the detectives was relatively painless. After the initial chiding, Willis had come straight out and told me that they were aware of my shaky history with the department, but that Chase had told them I was "good people." They filled the next thirty minutes with basic questions to which I could give only basic responses. I told them about the drug gang that wanted me dead, which peaked their interest.

"What's the name of this gang?" Kent asked.

"They don't have a name," I replied.

The detectives eyed me suspiciously, so I continued.

"It's part of their business model," I explained. "I'm sure you guys know how terrorists have been operating in independent cells so no one group knows too much about other operations. It helps keep Al Qaeda or ISIS leadership safe because there is no structured hierarchy to target."

The men nodded.

"Well, this group of Eastern European drug dealers has taken a different approach. They kept the basic hierarchical structure used by most organizations, but refused to take on an identity that could be helpful to law enforcement. Although most of them have plenty of ink, they don't all have a particular tattoo. They don't use gang signs and don't rely on an organization name to instill fear in their competition as has been done by MS-13 and the Aryan Brotherhood."

"How do they intimidate witnesses and handle the rest of their dirty work?" asked Willis.

"Enforcers," I said. "They have a few nameless enforcers who lack both identities and morals. They are incredibly brutal to the point even those in the organization fear them. If there is information to be extracted, or a rival to be eliminated, they get the call. The gang members are some of the worst human beings I've encountered. Enforcers are barely human. An enforcer gets assigned a task and then he slices and gouges his way through anybody who stands in the way. They don't stop. They never stop."

Willis wasn't writing. Kent wasn't reacting. They weren't buying it. I could see it in their eyes.

Kent said, "No offense, Mr. Galloway. But, it seems odd we've never been briefed on this. I mean everyone knows what happened to you, but we were told you were taken by a small group of dealers and that the group was taken out not long after you were rescued."

"That's how it's supposed to appear," I said. "Nobody looks for ghosts."

Willis chimed in and said, "So, you think the man who shot you may be one of these enforcers."

The more I thought about it, the more I thought it was unrelated. Too much just didn't make sense. The ethnic background was one thing, but there was another thing that bothered me more.

"I'm not sure," I said somberly. "There are a couple of problems with that theory."

"Like the shooter was of Hispanic descent," said Kent.

"Right. I don't think they'd bring in an outside hitter. They don't like too many moving parts. Things go wrong when they get complicated."

"And you are sure he appeared to be Hispanic?" Kent asked, not for the first time.

Throughout the interview, they had repeatedly quizzed me about nearly every detail. The only thing I'd never had to repeat was the model of the gun. Most cops know if there is anything a victim of a firearms crime can describe, it's the gun. The eyes always go to the gun. The mind captures the gun in full color and the image becomes etched in eternity.

"He was Hispanic," I confirmed.

"You said there were a couple of problems with the theory. What's the other one?" asked Willis.

My stomach turned and I remembered how the man had me dead to rights at close range.

"I'm still alive," I said. "Their enforcers don't leave anything to chance."

Willis scribbled in his notepad Kent put his hands in his pockets and sized me up.

Kent asked, "Again, I mean no offense, but, how do you know about these so-called enforcers? It seems like they may be the stuff of legends. Or, maybe more precisely, the stuff of myths."

I remembered back to a darkened room in a building far away from this city. The streets outside were covered in snow and a radiator was hissing in the corner. I had thought I was alone in the room, but I wasn't. I had tried to turn my back on death, but death had found me.

"I've met one," I said softly.

I'm not sure if a second or a minute passed before anyone spoke.

"During your undercover work?" asked Kent.

I shook my head. "Later. After I left the department."

Willis stopped writing and raised an eyebrow. "Are you

saying one of these guys came after you?"

The tone of the conversation was changing. The friendly detectives had taken Chase at his word, but their instincts were causing them to question my reliability. How much had they heard about me? Surely, they knew about my spiral into addiction. Did they know about the hallucinations? Did they know my life was filled with phantoms?

"Yes," I replied.

Willis asked, "If they are as ruthless as you claim, how are you still breathing?"

Claim. He said, claim. Not say, or said. *Claim.* I'd lost them. While I may have been inches away from the two men, my credibility was miles away.

"I got lucky," I mumbled.

Kent sniffed. "I'd say you did."

Willis tapped his pen against his cheek and said, "Have you run into any more of these enforcers?"

I thought about the two men who made a move on me when I'd left Planetary Electronics. They were members, but not enforcers. I can't explain how I knew. I'd only encountered one enforcer, but he had a *feel* to him. I'd heard rumblings others like him existed, but none had come after me thus far. Not on that day in Squirrel Hill and not in my house. If one was sent for me, I doubt anyone would see him coming.

For the next few minutes, I tried to steer the conversation back to my involvement with the Spartan investigation and how the shooter could have been linked to those efforts. However, I couldn't make any solid connections and the detectives became understandably bored by the disgraced, druggie detective with questionable people skills and even more questionable concepts of the word "real." They were cordial when they left, leaving me business cards and reassuring glances. The door swung open as they made their way into the hallway. Just as the door was closing, I saw my old dead enemy Lukas Derela grinning from the hallway.

Another twenty-four hours and one hundred illegible signatures later I was allowed to leave the hospital. The weather had turned colder, but Jackie had brought me a fresh set of clothing, including a thick maroon sweatshirt, one of my baseball hats, and a gray ski jacket. After we got into the car and she'd pulled into traffic, I took a closer look at the sweatshirt.

"Is this mine?"

She nodded.

"I thought I'd lost it," I said. Assuming she had retrieved it from my house when she's picked up the rest of my clothing, I asked, "Was it somewhere in the back of my closet?"

"No. It was at my place." she said.

I stopped trying to adjust the size of the baseball cap that stubbornly refused to fit around my bandaged head.

"You've had it all this time and didn't throw it away?"

She didn't say anything.

"Thank you," I said.

"For?"

"For not hating me."

"I do hate you," she said without sounding spiteful. "But I'm trying not to anymore. Loving you was taxing, but hating you costs just as much."

We stopped by a store and bought hair clippers before going to my place. Walking in the front door of my house, the smell of household cleaners hit my nostrils. My eyes found the spot where I'd fallen and bled.

"I did what I could to clean the carpet," Jackie said, her voice muted as if we'd entered a funeral home. "It won't completely come clean. You can try having it steam-cleaned."

The stain on the beige carpeting appeared ocular in shape as if the eye of the abyss was staring up into this world, seeking victims to pull into the depths of a dark past. The entryway to my home would never be the same, and no amount of cleaning, nor fresh carpeting would be able to erase the memory of what had happened. A man had entered my home, the closest thing I had to a sanctuary, and had shot me in the head. A stranger whom I had never harmed, burst through my front door and tried to end my life. Not only that, but I had little doubt he would have killed Jackie if she had been close enough to intervene.

"Trevor?"

I turned to speak to Jackie and realized my teeth were clenched. My hands were balled into fists, so tight I could have turned coal into diamonds. The muscles in my neck ached with tension and an emotion I knew all too well. I drew in air as heavy as syrup through my nostrils and my jaw slackened. My fingers stretched out from my palms and the knots in my muscles unwound.

"Yes," I said.

Jackie's eyes locked on mine and her expression went from concern to either affirmation or relief.

"There it is," she said with a smirk.

"What?" I asked.

"The lava."

"The lava?"

She said, "The underlying volatility."

"I don't understand," I lied. "I'm fine."

She let the topic drop and said, "Are you hungry?"

"I could eat," I said, looking back at the bloodstain.

"Good," she said while plopping down on the couch. "Make me something too. Worrying about you is exhausting."

* * *

Jackie left after lunch and I spent some time doing my best to temporarily secure my damaged front door, although it still wouldn't be able withstand much more than a hard knock from a solicitor. After I finished practicing doorway triage, I cut my hair to a length most Marines would call conservative, showered, and changed out the thick bandage for my head for a thinner version. I dressed in jeans, a long sleeve T-shirt, my black leather jacket, and a black Pirates cap. I tucked my Sig Sauer into the back of my waistband and clipped a folding Gerber knife onto one of the pockets of my jeans. At my desk, I used my computer to type out an official-looking document on what might pass for realty company letterhead, printed out the page, and stuffed it into an envelope. I wrote URGENT NOTICE on it, slid it inside my jacket and went to the kitchen to grab some recycling and headed out the door.

Twenty minutes later, I pulled up outside the apartment building of Roger "Stretch" Orta. I waited until I saw someone walking toward the main entrance before grabbing the full bags. Timing my approach just right, I ended up at the entrance as a black woman in her sixties punched a code into a keypad that would grant her access into the building. I rustled the plastic bags and made a show of struggling to carry my items. The woman glanced over her shoulder as she opened the door.

"Hi," I said as I made an exaggerated effort to lift an arm and punch in my code. I let one of the bags slip down my wrist and tried readjust to get my index finger on the keypad.

She flashed teeth as white as I've ever seen and said, "Oh, here you go." She held the door open and I thanked her between heavy breaths.

We walked to the elevators together and once we were in she asked me which floor I needed.

"Five, please," I said, remembering Stretch's address had him in apartment 502.

The woman pushed the buttons for five and seven and I thanked her again as I got off the elevator.

Dropping the bags in a corner of the hallway, I proceeded to walk to 502. Reaching inside my jacket, I retrieved the envelope slid it under the door, and knocked three times before shifting out of sight of the peephole. A few seconds later, I heard the door and then the rustling of the envelope being opened. Then I heard the same voice I'd heard on the intercom.

"Damn it! What the hell?" he said as he read the mock URGENT NOTICE regarding the supposed graffiti on his apartment door and how he was financially responsible for the removal.

The door flew open as he decided to check the exterior and I pushed my way inside the apartment before he knew what was happening.

"Hello, Stretch," I said as I gripped his shirt and forced him through a hallway. We cleared the hallway and entered a living room that was roughly the size of Montana. With a firm shove I knocked him down to the hardwood floor. Oak, I think. Extremely nice.

"Dude!" he exclaimed. "Who the—" his words trailed off as he recognized my face.

"We need to talk," I said while removing my hat to show my shaved and damaged head. He looked surprised, but not "hey, I thought you were dead" surprised.

"Christ," he said. "Did Keri do that to you? She really beat the crap out of you."

I squinted at him. Well, at least now I had the girl's real name.

"No. Your girlfriend didn't do this to me. Your Hispanic friend with the semiautomatic pistol did this to me."

He was perplexed. Or, at least he was doing a good job at faking confusion. Of course if he had taken acting lessons from his girlfriend Keri, then he could probably fool most anyone.

"You were *shot?*" said Stretch as he got to his feet.

"I was shot," I said.

Fighting the urge to say more, I stared him down and waited for him to react. Nothing in the world is as rare and as revealing as a deep, drawn-out period of accusatory silence. I allowed my dead, stoic eyes to penetrate his as the moment developed from what he must have thought would be fleeting, to uncomfortable, to unbearable. I made certain my gaze did not falter. Good investigators know when you own the silence, you own your adversary.

His eyes slipped to the side once, then again. After nearly a minute, he swallowed hard and cleared his throat. Ten seconds later, he spoke.

Holding his hands up in mock-surrender, a wide-eyed Stretch said, "Hey, man, I didn't have anything to do with you getting shot."

I didn't speak and remained still.

"I swear," he exclaimed. "I don't even know any Mexicans."

I was tempted to explain the difference between the terms "Hispanic" and "Mexican," but chose to let it go.

"I'm being straight with you! Gunplay isn't my thing, man."

He stood up straighter and did his best to convey toughness. "If I gotta straighten somebody out, I'll stand toe-to-toe with him and deliver an epic beatdown."

I took a step toward him and his posture withered. I said, "Or you'll send your girlfriend to deal with the problem."

"That wasn't nothin', man," he stammered. "I just wanted to know what was what. It wasn't anything personal. Keri said you wanted to talk about Jimmy. You wanna talk about Jimmy? We can talk about Jimmy."

I took another step into his personal space. "A bullet went through my head, Mr. Orta. To me, that topic takes priority."

He took half a step back and said, "I told you, man, I don't know anything about any guns. That's not the way I—"

I punched him in the throat. Without even thinking, I had folded the fingertips of my right hand toward the palm and created a wedge with my knuckles that was the perfect size to be able to strike someone in the Adam's apple. Then, I had lashed out hard enough to temporarily disrupt his breathing. He was shocked, but I was even more shocked. *Where the hell had that come from?*

With hands over his throat, he gasped in panic. Slowly, he regained the ability to breathe—as did I. I hoped my typical unreadability would pay off, and he wouldn't be able to tell how shaken I was that I'd lost control. I had no idea why I had punched him. I was playing the part of being stern and imposing, but the truth was I wasn't even sure I was actually angry. It was as if my brain had sent the order to keep my temper in check, but my arm hadn't gotten the memo.

"I...It wasn't me," Stretch gurgled.

"Then who?" I said, still trying to appear composed and confident.

"I have no idea," he said. "I don't have any reason to kill you, man."

"Unless you killed Jimmy."

He shook his head while rubbing his throat. His voice strengthened as he said, "No way, man. He was money."

"Meaning?"

"He was my paycheck, man. That's too much scratch to give up," he explained.

"You're extremely sentimental," I said dryly. "I can tell that Jimmy meant a lot to you."

"Jimmy was all right most the time, man. Other than being tight, he wasn't bad."

"Tight?"

Stretch eyed me warily and I could tell he was trying to decide how much he should say. I took an aggressive step closer.

"Wait," he yelled, taking a stride away from me. "I mean he paid well, but didn't pay me what I was worth. Jimmy was rolling in it but tossed me shit wages, in comparison. If I said anything about it, he'd say he could get anyone to flip some switches. That's what he said. 'Flip some switches.' This shit isn't easy, especially when the musician's talent has gone AWOL."

I looked him over and tried to imagine him bashing a hole in Jimmy's skull. The truth was, I could see him doing it if he were desperate enough. With some people, it takes less than thirty seconds to recognize murder isn't in the cards. With others, like Stretch, you can get the sense that feelings of desperation will breed a capacity for violence. I saw the potential in this man. However, as we stood in his massive apartment surrounded by expensive electronics, I did not sense desperation. I studied him and his gaze fell to the floor.

"Look at me," I said.

Reluctantly he raised his eyes and I examined them. I looked down at the skin on his arms. I called upon my years as a narcotics investigator to assimilate everything about the man in front of me. If he was an addict, I would know it. I would simply know. He wasn't. With no addiction and no obvious money problems, there were limited reasons why Stretch would be desperate enough to kill.

"What are you doing?" he said. "Why are out looking at me like that? You're freaking me out."

Once you take a desperate need for money out of the equation, the other reason most people are willing to kill for is obvious.

"Your girlfriend's name is Keri, right?"

He nodded.

"What's her last name?"

"Wilk."

"When did Jimmy first make a play for her?"

"What?" he asked.

"Jimmy tried to move in on Keri, right? That must have pissed you off."

He scrunched up his eyebrows.

"Come on," I said. "Jimmy was twice her age. There was no way you could let that stand."

"When?" he asked. His breathing increased and he blurted out, "She never said anything. Not one word. I thought they barely knew each other."

I watched him for any signs of deception, but saw none. Sometimes, working an investigation is like completing a maze on a piece of paper. You move your pen down a path, hit a dead end, and immediately retrace the path before heading down an alternative route. However, trial and error doesn't work long. If you scroll your pen down too many incorrect routes, all you get is a jumbled mess that is impossible to navigate. I had to think this through.

I backed away from Stretch and started to pace the hardwood floor in his expansive living room. With each slow stride, I did my best to examine the facts objectively.

"What are you doing?" Stretch asked.

I turned my head his direction, put a finger to my lips, and kept walking while working it out in my mind.

Fact: Stretch had been avoiding me.

Fact: He sent his girlfriend to gather intelligence, meaning he had something to hide.

Assumption: Stretch was not desperate enough to kill.

Fact: He seems to be clueless about the man who shot me.

Fact: He doesn't think Jimmy was paying him what he was worth.

Fact: He doesn't like direct conflict and prefers deception.

Assumption: If he felt he was being shortchanged by Jimmy, he would attempt to rectify the situation without confronting Jimmy.

Fact: Stretch has expensive taste and has no visible money problems.

Assumption: He found a way to increase his income at Jimmy's expense.

I stopped walking and turned his direction.

"Did you take an expensive turntable from Jimmy's game room?"

"No," he said after a pause that was ever so slight.

"Stretch…" I said.

"I swear, man. I didn't take any record player!"

"Turntable," I corrected.

"I didn't take anything from his house. Nothing."

That was interesting. He specified that he hadn't taken anything *from the house*. He didn't say that he hadn't taken anything from Jimmy. The way he'd answered the question gave me hope that another theory I had was valid.

"What's was your angle?" I asked. "You were stealing from Jimmy and that's what you're hiding."

He shook his head a little too emphatically.

"I'm investigating a murder," I said. "Not theft. But, until I completely understand your role here, you're a suspect."

Stretch opened his eyes wide and said, "Whoa! Slow

your roll! Why me?"

"Because you dodged me, got your girlfriend to work me for information, and you've already admitted you had motive because you thought Jimmy didn't pay you well enough."

I knew what I was saying was weak, but it's all in the presentation.

I raised my voice an octave and said, "Then when you decided I was getting too close, you send your buddy to my house to put a bullet in my head."

I was full of it and I knew it.

"That puts you on the hook for both murder and attempted murder," I said jabbing a finger into his chest. "Since you haven't given me anything else, then that has to be what you're hiding." Pulling out my phone, I said, "Did I mention I used to be a Pittsburgh cop? Let me call my buddies to let them know I'm in the same room with the man who killed Jimmy Spartan. Whether or not you get convicted, I'm sure scores of musicians will be looking to hire you once you're charged with killing an industry legend."

Stretch squeaked, "Hey, there's no need for all of that. I don't need to be dealing with any murder cops."

I held the phone in front of his face and said, "What was your racket?"

He stepped away from me and started doing some pacing of his own.

"Merchandising, man."

"Explain," I demanded.

He exhaled and rubbed his hands on his head.

"I wasn't just Jimmy's sound engineer. I coordinated all the merchandising and handled everything from the online T-shirt sales to the merch booths at concerts. The inventory, the tracking, the graphics...that's my gig. I get the people the stuff they want for a reasonable price."

"How long have you been skimming?" I asked.

He put his hands in his pockets and looked down. "Three years."

I figured that meant five.

"So, when I first showed up here and told you that Jimmy's family had asked me to look into some things, you thought your scheme was blown."

"Yeah," he said softly.

"How much have you taken from Jimmy over the years?"

"Not much," he said. "Ten...maybe fifteen grand."

I concluded two things: He had netted upward of twenty thousand and that Mr. Roger "Stretch" Orta and I had vastly different definitions of the word "much." I didn't know a lot about the music industry, but I knew enough about corporate practices to know when a money-making body hits the ground, the vultures don't waste any time in circling.

I asked, "With Jimmy gone, why haven't the record label lawyers swooped in to assume control of the business end?"

He shrugged. Then, I realized what Stretch had been up to. While explaining what he'd been doing, he had been swinging back and forth between present and past tense. He *had* been in charge of merchandise sales and concerts but was still able to *get the people the stuff they want.*

"Ah, I see." I said. "The record labels came in and took over the legitimate sales, but you're still running unlicensed products. With the bump in popularity after Jimmy's death, I bet you've done extremely well both domestically and overseas."

Again, he shrugged.

"Assuming most of your sales have been through the internet and shipments have been crossing state lines, you're staring down some serious federal time, Stretch."

Finally, I wasn't guessing or bluffing. I had him and he knew it.

"Can you help me out?" he said. "I need a deal."

Now it was my turn to shrug. "You need to have something to get something, Stretch. From where I'm standing, your hands are empty."

His face was white and all of his bravado had fled the premises. He was scared and he was right to be. Stretch was no tough guy and he'd be a chew toy in prison.

"You asked me about a turntable," he said.

Apparently, I had been right when I'd sensed he knew something about the missing item. However, no prosecutor would trade a stupid turntable for sure conviction.

"What about it?" I asked coolly.

"I might know something about it. In fact, I might have a good idea who killed Jimmy."

"Bullshit," I said profoundly.

"I'm serious," he said. "But, I'm not saying anything more until I have a deal. Talk to your cop friends or whatever lawyers you need to, but I'd think catching the killer of the famous Jimmy Spartan is worth something."

I didn't completely believe him, but I didn't completely disbelieve him either. I crossed my arms and thought it through. Murder always trumps white collar crime and while Stretch may have been smart enough to have his larceny go undetected for several years, I couldn't see him living the life of a fugitive on the run. If he did run, he'd eventually get caught or get himself killed by ripping off the wrong people.

I started dialing my phone.

"Wait. Just wait," Stretch pleaded.

I held up a hand and he flinched as if I was going to hit him. Again, something twisted in my gut as I wondered why I'd hit him the first time.

"Relax, kid. I'm calling a friend. I don't have a direct line of communication to the District Attorney or the U.S.

Attorney. I've got a friend in the department who may be able to get the conversation started."

I dialed Chase, got his voicemail, and left a message. Although he was not the lead investigator on the Spartan case, nor a fraud investigator, he would be able to grease the wheels to get Stretch at the same table with the right detectives and somebody from the DA's office.

Stretch asked, "Now what?"

"Now, we wait for my friend to return my call."

He glanced at his watch and said, "I have to go."

"The hell you do," I said. "We're staying put until we hear back from Detective Vinson and then you'll have a long evening of conversations ahead of you."

"You don't understand," he said. "I have to take care of something and then I can meet with your friend and who- ever else I need to see."

"You must be kidding," I said. "You just admitted to multiple felonies and claimed to have knowledge about a homicide. I have no doubt that you possess a decent amount of common sense, so you must realize you aren't cut out to live the life of a fugitive. You'll be hunted down, your girl- friend will be scrutinized as an accessory, and there won't be any deal that will keep you from doing serious time in a penitentiary. When you run from something like this, you aren't simply crossing a bridge. You're burning it behind you and there is no going back."

He shook his head vigorously. "It's not that, man. It's my mom. She's disabled and can't get around on her own. She counts on me to drive her to the store, fix things around her house and pay her bills. I'm supposed to be picking her up right now. She's expecting me to install a new thermo- stat in her house and then take her to the grocery store. I swear, I'm on the level."

"Even if that were true," I said. "I'm sure you can get

someone else to help her today."

"It's true!" he said. "And there's nobody else." He shuffled his feet, looked down, and said, "I don't have a lot of friends and we don't have any other family. It's just me and her."

He seemed sincere, but after having been fooled by his girlfriend, I was doubtful.

"If you don't believe me, I can call her right now," he said. "I'll put the call on speaker and you can listen."

I decided to call his bluff and told him to make the call. Sure enough, Mamma Stretch was wondering why her son was late and had a list of chores for him to accomplish. He told his mother he'd been held up and hoped to be on the way shortly. He hung up and looked at me expectantly.

"Then, I'm your new best friend," I said. "I'm tagging along and keeping you under my thumb."

Stretch groaned, "Come on, man. She's disabled, not stupid. It will take her all of two seconds to know we aren't friends. You aren't exactly...I mean, you don't seem like..."

He had a point, but letting him roam free wasn't an option. Of course, it was starting to occur to me that I wasn't a cop anymore and I really didn't have any authority to make Stretch do a damn thing. Hopefully, he wouldn't come to the same realization anytime soon. However, if I insisted on keeping him at my side, he might very well decide to go his own way and force me into a situation where if I tried to keep him in one place I could be charged with abduction.

"Then I'm tailing you," I compromised. "Consider me your shadow for the day." I'll stay in behind you and flash my lights when I hear from Detective Vinson. "But, if you try to run, all bets are off. Understand?"

"You have my word," he said.

My muscles immediately tensed. It's been my experience that when a criminal verbally gives you his word, that word isn't worth the paper it's not written on.

TRACK 9
"A SHEEP IN WOLF'S CLOTHING"

I pulled behind Stretch's Lexus, and followed him as he made his way down the hills from Highland Park. We followed the Allegheny River before turning south toward his mother's home in Monroeville, I watched the back of Stretch's head and our eyes periodically met in his rearview. I checked my own and confirmed we were not being followed by the living and my backseat was not occupied by the dead. I tried to push thoughts about my hallucinations of Lukas Derela out of my mind as I kept watch on the car ahead of me. Even from behind, I could tell Stretch was periodically tapping his hands on the steering wheel and mouthing the words to a song.

Stretch pulled into a driveway off Poplar Street and I continued down until I could find a place to turn around. I pointed my Jetta back in the direction of the house and found a spot where I could set up on the small, white, single-story house. As I threw the car in park, I witnessed Stretch bound up three wooden steps onto a porch to be greeted by an elderly lady with a cane. My phone rang as he disappeared inside the house. The caller ID told me it was Chase.

"Are you busy?" I asked.

"I've been busier," he answered. "What's up?"

I told him about my conversation with Stretch, leaving

out the parts about me being guilty of a home invasion and an assault. I figured all of that would eventually come up, but why toil over the details now?

"Where are you?" he asked.

"I'm outside his mom's house in Monroeville. He's inside with her but I have no way of making him stay if he decides to bolt." I gave Chase the address.

"I'll call Monroeville P.D. and get one of their detectives to meet with you now. I should be there within forty-five minutes," he said. "Stall him if he tries to go anywhere, but don't do anything illegal. There are still plenty of cops around here who would love to stick it to you."

"You know me," I said.

"Yeah, some days I do," he replied and then the call went dead.

Thirty minutes later, I looked over my steering wheel to see a black Dodge Charger crawling down Poplar in my direction. More and more cops were finding themselves riding around in the Charger as Ford and Chevy seemed to struggle maintain production of police vehicles that were acceptable to departments. This one was unmarked and, in spite of the glare on the windshield, I could make out the shape of only one person inside. The spot I was in was not exactly inconspicuous, so I waited for the detective to see me and approach, but the investigator surprised me by stopping short and turning into the driveway. Either the detective or Chase had misunderstood me and thought we were meeting at the house.

I started my car as somebody got out of the Charger and approached the front door. I was a football field away and couldn't see much more than a bulky form climb the porch steps. I put the car into drive, and paused when I saw the detective seemingly walk through the front door without even knocking. I pressed the accelerator and was nearly to the driveway when I recognized the distinct sound of gun-fire coming from the direction of the house.

I pressed the gas pedal to the floor and then slammed the brakes when I reached the driveway and the Jetta skidded to a stop, blocking most of the wide driveway. I leapt out, drew my gun, and started moving toward the hood of my car when I heard the sound of squeaking hinges. My Volkswagen was still between me and the house when the front door of the house flew completely open and there stood the same man who had shot me in the head. A Glock dangled at his side as our eyes met.

The stranger squinted as if he didn't believe his eyes.

"I already killed you," he said in an accented voice. The tone he used in making the statement wasn't one of great amazement. His eyes didn't widen and his jaw didn't drop. In fact, his manner was every bit as passionate as a dirty shoelace. It was as if he had been checking off items on a shopping list and he had ended my life right after throwing milk and bread into his cart. I simply wasn't supposed to be there. I wasn't supposed to be anywhere.

"Drop the weapon," I commanded while raising my gun.

He pursed his lips and continued staring at me. His expression drifted from matter-of-fact, to one of disappointment. If I hadn't known any better, I would have sworn he was chastising himself for not successfully murdering me in my home.

"Now," I said.

"I already killed you," he repeated.

I made sure the sights of my pistol were lined up on his chest. I let the front sight blur in-between the shapes of the rear sights. My index finger was applying about five pounds of pressure on a trigger with a six-pound pull. My breathing was slow and my hands were steady. In this state, I was unflappable and lethal.

"Do it!" a voice hissed from behind me.

I felt Lukas Derela's breath on my neck. His long hair dangled in my peripheral vision, causing me to lose focus on the gun sights.

"You did not give me this much of a chance," he said. "Shoot already. It is what you do, is it not?"

"Shut up," I said softly.

The stranger on the porch glared at me in confusion. I shifted and did my best to concentrate on the task at hand, which was not talking to the man I killed years ago.

"Why have you not pulled the trigger?" Derela asked. "Are you afraid of making another mistake?"

"You weren't a mistake, you bastard," I insisted. He continued as if he didn't hear me. His lips were practically pressed to my ear but I dared not take my eyes of the man with the Glock.

"Or is it something else?" he asked. He craned his neck around my head and whispered into my other ear. "Did you lose your nerve? Did you lose your fire? Did not anyone tell you? It is the fire that keeps the wolves at bay. Can you hear them out there? They are coming for you and then you will be mine. You will be with me and what a feast of you will I make." He growled and snapped his teeth. The perplexed man on the porch took one step down toward the yard.

"Stop," I yelled to the man. "Stop," I said to Derela.

The man took another step. Derela said another word.

"Mistake," he said.

"Killing you wasn't a mistake," I said.

Now as if in the distance I heard the words, "Not *that* mistake." Without looking, I knew the hallucination was gone.

The man took another step.

The chill in the air did nothing to prevent sweat from

forming on my forehead. The muscles in my forearm contracted and my grip around the pistol tightened. My pulse quickened and my breaths sounded heavy. My unflappable and lethal posture had lost at least one of those components and possibly both.

Why couldn't Derela leave me the hell alone? Why couldn't his people, real or not, stop stalking me? What more did I have to do to rid myself of past threats? How many more battles did I have to fight in a war I had never wanted? What the fuck did I do to deserve an addiction-plagued life where my choices are mind-dulling pills or death by a thousand mirages?

The man took another step.

My thoughts raged.

People are often criticized for having a lack of self-awareness. But, I'm fucking self-aware. I know what I stand for and what I won't stand for. I understand my demons, know where they live, and knock on their doors asking for a fair fight. And what do they do? They sneak up behind me when I'm in a standoff with man who kicked in the door of my home with the sole intent of putting bullet in my head. And for what? To what end? He was willing to take my life for reasons I don't fully understand and now that I was looking into his eyes, I was certain he would have killed Jackie without hesitation or remorse. Fuck that. Fuck him.

The man took another step and was in the yard.

I put four rounds into the center of his chest. His gun fell silently to the dying autumn grass. His expression was one of puzzlement yet acceptance.

As he dropped to his knees and took his last breaths, he said again, "I already killed you."

I walked toward him, keeping my gun trained on him the entire time.

He fell onto his back, looked up at me, and for the fourth time he said, "I already killed you."

Looking down at him, I said, "Yeah. I know how you feel."

"Did he say anything else? Anything at all?" Chase said as he knelt down next to the stranger's body.

A few feet away, a Monroeville detective's radio cracked as more marked patrol cars arrive on the scene. The detective, a clean-cut flagpole of a man named Craig Aymar, had already questioned me at length and confiscated my weapon. He was less than impressed with my answers when I told him and Chase all I knew about Roger "Stretch" Orta and his crimes. Aymar listened intently to the radio traffic and while scribbling on a notepad.

"Nothing," I replied.

Aymar stepped forward and slid a notebook into his jacket. "Tell me again why you were attempting to babysit this Roger Orta fella rather than letting the real police handle things?"

Chase stood. "Come on, Craig. He couldn't keep Stretch from going anywhere and he was having trouble getting in touch with me. He compromised the best he could."

"Yeah, well he has a history of compromising, doesn't he? From what I've heard, he's 'compromised' quite a few people before."

Chase took a step toward the man. I held up a hand and got in front of the moving mountain.

"It's okay," I said. "He's doing his job. I could have handled this better."

"You're damn right," said Aymar. "Now we have two bodies inside that house and—if you can be believed—they were killed by this man," the detective pointed to the stranger's corpse. "Who, by the way, is not carrying any identification and is driving a car with stolen plates."

"Did you run the VIN of the Charger?" I asked, referring to the Vehicle Identification Number that would be etched into at least two locations on the car.

"Dispatch just came back with the results," the detective sneered. "I have some great news, hotshot. Not only do we not have an ID on the man you killed, but the car he was driving had no paperwork inside and the VIN comes back 'not on file.' The car looks brand new and I wouldn't be surprised if it is fresh off of a dealership lot. The thing is, the man you shot had the key and the car hasn't been reported stolen. So...do you see that Dodge Charger sitting there? I thought I saw it, but I must not," he said, sarcastically. "I don't see it, because *that* 2018 Dodge Charger is not registered to anyone and isn't stolen." Pointing a finger to the car and then the body, he continued, "As of right now, neither that car nor that body have names assigned to them. Of course, we're going to run this dead guy's prints, so maybe we'll learn something from those results."

"I doubt it," I said. "I think he's a pro."

The more I had thought about it, the more confident I felt that the stranger was a professional hitter. If he had prints on file, there was a chance they were attached to a slew of aliases and his real identity would be nearly impossible to ascertain.

"I really don't care what you think," said Aymar. "For all I know, you gunned him down in cold blood and planted the gun after the fact. Not one person managed to corroborate your story that he raised a gun in your direction."

I tried to think of something to say. I should have been indignant, but the truth was that my truth was fiction. What was I supposed to do? Should I have waited until the man raised the gun an inch? Six inches? Most people don't realize the speed with which someone can raise a weapon and fire. Aside from that, criminals are often more accurate with their shots than the good guys since they don't worry about things like giving the proper verbal warnings or inadvertently hitting someone in the background. When confronted by mortal danger, you strike first or you get struck down. I did what I had to with Derela and I did the same with the murderer lying in front of me now.

"Are you charging him with anything, Craig?" Chase asked.

"Not right now."

"Then we're leaving," said Chase, placing a guiding hand on my shoulder.

On the walk to my car, I said, "He didn't give me a choice."

"I know. You did what you had to do. I might wonder about some things if you were being the old you, but now that you're Mr. Chill, I know you waited until the last second to plug him."

"Right," I said.

"Right," said Chase after a beat.

We arrived at the door of my car and Chase said, "This isn't your fault."

"Don't you ever get tired of saying that?"

"It's true," he said. "You couldn't have known this guy would track you here, assume you were inside and kill Stretch and his mother."

I had started opening the door to my car, but froze. Something was wrong.

"He didn't track me," I said. "I wasn't followed and I checked my car for tracking devices before I left the house this morning. There is no way he tracked me."

Chase was skeptical. "The hitter had already made one run at you. As far as you know, did he have any connection to Stretch?"

"No," I said. "But he had no known connection to me until he shot me in the head."

Chase asked, "Then why would this guy show up here out of the blue?"

I put my hands on the roof of the car and bowed my head. None of this made any sense. If I wasn't being tracked, then perhaps Stretch was. But, why hit him here and now? Slowly, the picture came into focus as I remembered the drive from Stretch's apartment.

"It wasn't out of the blue," I said. "Stretch made a call from his car. He had been mouthing words in his car and drumming his hands on the wheel, so I thought he was rapping or singing. Now, I think the drumming was a ruse and he was having a conversation."

Chase asked, "Who would he call?"

"That idiot," I said, shaking my head in disbelief. "That greedy idiot."

"Care to share?"

"Stretch told me he might have information about who killed Jimmy Spartan. I think he decided to use that information to blackmail someone into giving him enough money to run and start a new life. He called someone and threatened to talk if he didn't get paid in a big way. Whoever it was on the other end of that phone probably said they would pay up and even offered to send someone to take care of me in the process. Stretch gave this address, but had no idea the hitter would try to take everyone out."

"So, do you think the guy you just shot killed Jimmy Spartan?"

"I doubt it," I said. "Jimmy was killed with a blow to the head and it's pretty obvious that this guy preferred to keep it simple and use his gun."

"We still have to consider the possibility that somehow

you were followed and the hitter is in town for a contract job, sponsored by your Eastern European friends."

He was right. If I knew anything it was that I didn't know enough. It was still conceivable the hitter could have been hired by my old enemies. A more likely scenario was that the shooter was in business with Stretch. Stretch may have called his partner to warn him the walls were coming down and got a bullet for his trouble. Of course, there was still the loose tie-in with my visit to Planetary Electronics, the Peruvian counterfeiting operation, and this shooter who happened to be of Hispanic descent. The accomplice angle made the most sense, and I said so to Chase.

"Well if it was just the two of them ripping off Jimmy, then it's over," he reasoned.

I had assumed Stretch's scheme was limited in scope, but now I had my doubts. If he happened to have been working with someone else who wanted to tie up loose ends, then we had another problem.

"We need to find the girl," I said.

"Which girl?"

"Stretch's girlfriend."

"The one who beat you up?" Chase said with a grin.

"She didn't..." I began before realizing I was wasting my breath. "Her name is Keri Wilk. It's possible she could be in danger."

"Okay. I'll go track her down. You go home and take a load off."

"No way," I said. "I'll go—"

"Nope," Chase interrupted. "You just shot a man, your gun is evidence, and you are not a licensed PI. You're my friend, but I'm not losing my job because you can't sit the bench every once in a while. I've already got some explaining to do about why I'm involved in this whole mess and if I take you around town to knock on doors, my balls will be hanging on the chief's office wall. No thank you."

I wasn't thrilled, but I couldn't argue his point.

"Nice shooting, by the way," said Chase as he stood in V of the car door. "That was a tight pattern."

I didn't thank him because it felt like a compliment I didn't want.

"Before we go, do you think you can get Aymar to check Stretch's phone records and see who he called from the car?" I asked.

"Yeah, if he stops being a dick," said Chase.

"You can't blame him," I said. "He's got three dead bodies and the last man standing is a disgraced former cop who has more questions than answers."

"Whatever," Chase mumbled.

After a moment of quiet, I looked up at my friend. "A minute ago, did I hear you say I *plugged* the hitter? *Plugged?*"

Chase smiled.

"You seriously have to stop watching the classic movie channel," I said.

"Nonsense," said the tattooed-covered cop with the Chihuahua named Cujo. "You can't go wrong with the classics."

"What I'm hearing you say is that you had no choice in the matter."

"I didn't," I said.

"But, I'm sensing you feel some level of guilt."

I leaned back on the couch and looked at the ceiling. The familiar clock on the wall, the same one I saw in my recent nightmare, ticked away.

"I took a life," I said. "Of course I feel guilty."

Dr. Welch said, "So, that's how you feel after the fact.

How did you feel at the time of the incident?"

I answered, but the delay before the response was telling.

"My training kicked in and I reacted to the threat," I answered.

"You're lying," she observed, but spoke with no animosity. I brought my eyes down to meet hers. She smiled and said, "Is it possible your temper is returning? At least in short bursts?"

I didn't respond.

She said, "The guilt you feel for taking a life might be amplified if you took that life out of anger."

"I wasn't angry at this guy. At least not an intense anger," I explained. "First, I hit Roger Orta and didn't even realize I was doing it at the time. Then, while I was facing down the man who shot me, Derela showed up."

She leaned back, her face filled with concern. "Your hallucination of Lukas Derela appeared?"

I nodded.

"How often have you seen him lately?"

I told her about seeing him in the backseat of my car and catching a glimpse of him at the hospital.

"So, today makes three times?"

"Yes."

"How did you feel when that hallucination appeared today?"

"Tense."

"Tense?" she asked.

"Yes. Tense."

"But, not angry?"

"I'm controlling the anger," I said.

She put pen to paper and started writing.

I said, "You don't believe me. You think I'm reverting back to my old ways."

She stopped writing and said, "I don't know, Trevor. But,

I'm curious as to why you are so certain your old ways are so terrible. Obviously, you don't want to relapse and fall victim to your addiction. But, were your old ways really so bad?"

It was funny. Until she had mentioned my addiction, I hadn't realized that the temptation, while ever-present, had become an autumn whisper as opposed to a banshee scream. The stressors in my life may have been taking a toll on me, but the call of the needle was on the distant horizon rather than inches from my face.

"You know that my temper has caused me some problems. It got me kicked out of college, and I've hurt others since," I said.

"All of us have had to deal with anger issues. While you may have a propensity toward violence in those moments, I don't think you are being completely fair to yourself."

"Today, I nearly crushed one man's esophagus and put four hollow point rounds into another man's chest and I still don't feel as if I truly lost my temper."

"And that scares you," she observed.

"What happens when I snap?"

"*If*," she corrected. "Not *when* you snap. I think we can work through this. You have to find the balance between passion and rage. An individual can experience all of life's emotions, including anger and not react inappropriately."

"You mean violently," I said.

She wrote something down.

After a few seconds she said, "Perhaps it's time for you to anticipate the presence of potential stressors in your life and visualize how you are going to deal with them should they arise."

"Such as?" I asked.

"I don't know what is going on in your mind."

"You know you do," I said, looking away.

I heard her click the pen in her hand and drop her notebook on the floor. I turned my head to look at her. She was gorgeous and bright and too insightful. She could see through me like no other.

"Right now, in this moment, what is it that frightens you, Trevor?"

My thoughts swirled with drugs, guns, knives, criminals, phantoms and badges. I formulated my answer. Deep down, I knew there were two things that scared me most.

I feared that I would lose everything.

I feared that I would have nothing to lose.

Dr. Welch said, "You are concerned about outcomes that are far from certain. But, to a large extent, not only do you control what you may lose, but you can redefine what is important in your life."

I hadn't realized I'd spoken my fears aloud, but I had to admit her analysis made sense. Maybe I was worrying too much. So I punched a thief and shot a man who clearly wanted me dead. I'd reacted naturally. Even rationally. If I felt a flicker of the old fire, then so be it. What was it Derela had said? "Fire keeps the wolves at bay?" As long as the campfire didn't flash over and burn down the entire forest, then I would be fine. Everything would be fine.

Jackie came by the house later that evening. As soon as I opened the door and saw her face, I knew she'd heard about the shooting.

"Let me guess," I said. "Chase called you."

She shrugged off her coat and I hung it over the back of a chair in the living room.

"He didn't have to. Channel Two reported there were three dead bodies in Monroeville and a former Pittsburgh detective was somehow involved. Since you haven't been answering your phone, I knew it had to be you. Then, I called Chase and he told me what happened." She put her hands on her hips and said, "What the hell, Trevor? I've been worried sick. You should have called to let me know what happened. Where have you been for the last few hours?"

I put my hand on her face and stroked her cheek. "You are absolutely right. Not calling was selfish and it's inexcusable. I suppose I've gotten used to thinking that nobody but Chase is worrying about me, but that's not a good enough reason for me to not have called."

Her eyes softened and she asked, "Have you just been sitting around here?"

"I met with my therapist," I said. "I have a lot to sort out."

Jackie reached up and put her hand around the one I had on her face and gave it a gentle squeeze and we lowered our hands together.

"I don't know where we are going, Trevor. But, I know I don't want to lose you again."

I leaned down and we kissed. She let her fingers find the back of my neck and slide up. She stopped kissing me and pulled away a few inches.

Lightly tapping the back of my shaved head, she said, "I'm going to have to get used to that. I'd like to be around you enough to get used to that."

I smiled. I actually smiled.

We made love, and then lay in bed as the sun set outside the bedroom window.

"I've been cleared," she said. "I'm going back to work."

"That was fast," I said.

"Well, there isn't anyone to dispute my account, and you and Nick corroborated my story."

"Nick?"

She stretched underneath the sheets. "You remember my partner, Nick."

"Right."

The memory of the excitement down the street from Planetary Electronics reminded that I needed to broach an uncomfortable subject with Jackie.

"Jackie," I said, propping myself up on an elbow. "I need to talk to Vince."

She stopped stretching and her head turned slowly in my direction. "I know you don't mean Vince Sonta."

I waited.

"Trevor, you can't go near him. You've already come close to blowing this operation and my bosses will nail you to the wall if you get within five hundred feet of that place. While I've been on suspension, there's been an increase in traffic in and out of that building. Sonta has a lot of new help."

"What new help?" I asked.

"Vince's old crew seems to have been replaced by some serious hard cases. We aren't sure, but from the photos I've seen, these guys aren't technical support. They look like muscle and carry themselves like players. Nick saw Vince's son Tom down on the sidewalk getting pushed around by a few of them while Vince stood in the window and watched. Activity is escalating and you can't be caught in the middle. As it stands, you're lucky you haven't been charged with obstruction of justice, especially since you aren't licensed."

"I know I'm treading water here," I said. "But I can't shake the feeling that the man I shot today could have somehow been tied to Vince."

Somewhere in the back of my damaged head, I kept replaying my conversation with Vince. He'd told me something that somehow seemed relevant to the man I'd shot, but I couldn't put my finger on what it was.

Jackie adjusted my pillow—her pillow—and said, "That doesn't make any sense. What possible link could there be between the two?"

I had to admit that any lines I could connect between a man who I believed might be a paid assassin and a suspected counterfeiting operation were nebulous at best.

"He was Hispanic," I said weakly.

Jackie touched my bare chest and said, "You know as well as I do that it's probably a coincidence. If the guy was a pro, he could have ties to a drug cartel, MS-13, or a dozen other gangs with Hispanic members. You asked Vince about a record player. That's it."

"Turntable."

Jackie sighed, got up and started gathering her clothes from the floor.

"You aren't staying?"

She smiled. "I told you, I'm going back to work."

"Yeah, but I didn't know you meant tonight."

"We have new players to follow around and we're bumping up our surveillance operations," she explained while getting dressed. "Starting tonight, we're keeping an eye on Vince, Tom, and the new henchmen round the clock. I get to experience the joys of sitting in my cold car and watching the outside of one of the newbie's motel rooms while he sleeps soundly inside."

"Henchmen? Have you been watching old detective movies with Chase?"

She laughed. "No, but I do love the classics. If hats were still in style you could use one to cover your bandage. It would be a good look for you."

She rose to go.

"Want some company?" I asked.

The look she gave me cut a new gorge into my skull.

"Stay away from anything related to Planetary Electronics," she reminded me. "Something has the hive stirred up and it has nothing to do with Jimmy Spartan or drug gangs. This is in my wheelhouse and you need to stay clear until this is finished. Okay?"

"Okay," I said.

She finished putting on her shirt and looked down at me. "You seem different today."

"What do you mean?"

She cocked her head. "You seem the same."

"I think that bullet must have hit my brain after all."

"No...I mean you seem a little bit more like your old self. The good parts, anyway."

She waked out and I let myself doze off. My dreams didn't include any dead drug dealers or musicians dangling from bridges. For the first time in years, I dreamed of a future rather than the past.

For some reason, I woke from one of my dreams and the clock on the nightstand told me it was a quarter after three in the morning. I got up to use the restroom and was slinking back into bed when something caught my attention. I knew it was likely my imagination, but I thought I smelled cigarette smoke. I pulled on a pair of boxer shorts and walked through the dark house without my gun, which was now in the capable hands of Detective Aymar. The front door was closed and was still secured, if you could call it that, by a hook and eye mechanism. To be safe, especially since my gun was in the hands of Detective Aymar of the Monroeville PD, I decided I should prop one of the kitchen chairs against the door. My bare feet had just touched the linoleum in the kitchen when I realized I wasn't alone. Enough light from the street made its way through the window over the sink to allow me to make out the silhouette of a man sitting at the table. I froze and realized I could hear his breathing. Although I couldn't see his features, and could not be certain he was real, I did know two things without a doubt. The man was not my invented embodiment of Lukas Derela, and he was a malevolent being.

"Good evening, Mr. Galloway."

His voice was unfamiliar, but the way he said the "v" in "evening" hinted that he was fighting the desire to pronounce the sound as a "w."

"Good evening," I responded taking a step forward. Immediately, another man emerged from the shadows in the corner of the room, racked a shotgun, and pointed it at my chest.

"Subtle," I said.

The man at the table inhaled from a cigarette and the red tip glowed enough that I could see the weathered landscape of his face and hands. This man—or phantom—had more years behind him than ahead.

"Do you know who I am?"

"No."

"My name is Pavel Nekovar."

Now I was *really* hoping this was a hallucination.

Something must have shown in my expression because he said, "You know the name?"

"I've heard it mentioned."

He took another drag from the cigarette. "Please, sit down."

I took a seat at the opposite end of the table and did a quick scan for anything I might be able to reach and use as a weapon. Unless the crime boss was a slug that could be melted by the contents of a salt shaker, I was out of luck.

"I am certain you are aware that I am affiliated with the institution you have offended."

"Could you narrow it down?" I asked. "I've offended a

lot of institutions lately. Did I forget to renew my zoo membership? I do love the penguin parades they have in the winter."

"Szymon, would you mind helping Mr. Galloway focus?" asked the old man as he gave a nod to the man with the shotgun.

Szymon lowered the shotgun and leaned it against the wall behind him. I glanced back to Nekovar and before I knew what was happening, I was on the floor convulsing uncontrollably. I wasn't experiencing a hallucination. I was experiencing an electrocution.

When the current stopped flowing through my body, I was looking up at a Taser being held by a sneering Szymon.

"Is he conscious?" I heard the old man say.

"Tak," said Szymon.

I heard the sound of a chair being slid across the floor and the next thing I knew Nekovar was sitting next to me. He tapped a cane next to my head.

"Do you wish to play any more games, Mr. Galloway?"

I shook my head, or thought I did.

"After the failed attempt on your life, I have been asked to visit this city and oversee operations. It seems my predecessor has displeased those in power and I am to assume his duties until a suitable replacement can be found."

I managed to say, "That's very corporate of you."

Szymon kicked me in the ribs and I cursed. Throughout my time working narcotics, the name Pavel Nekovar had been tied to the rust belt drug trade but usually closer to Detroit and Cleveland. If he'd been sent this far south, there had to have been some sort of shake up.

"Although I was not involved with previous events, I have been told you are a hard man to kill. In fact, you have eliminated some of our best. Yet, here you are on the floor and your life is in my hands. How can this be?"

"Get it over with," I said.

The old man looked at me with curiosity. "You will not beg?"

"I will not beg."

"You will not bargain?"

"No."

The cane struck me across the nose, causing my eyes to water. When the tears receded from my eyes, I looked back at the man. I wasn't scared as much as I was interested in what was coming next. Nekovar was rumored to be an extremely powerful man in the organization that wanted me dead. So, why was he here? He could have simply sent Szymon or one of a dozen other brutes he had on the payroll. Why the personal attention rather than a clean hit like what had been attempted on me in Squirrel Hill? Or had he been referring to the Hispanic professional in my house? Exactly which failed attempt was he referencing?

Nekovar must have picked up on my interest, because he leaned over top of me, the curious expression fixed into place.

"You will not beg or ask for a deal, yet you do not seem particularly upset. Men enter your home and beat you, and this does not make you want to lash out. You do not simmer with anger?"

I didn't say anything. I still had too many questions rolling around in my head.

"You fascinate me, Mr. Galloway. That is why I asked management to allow me to speak with you rather end your life."

"What do you want?"

"Access," said the man. "Only a little access."

"To?"

"Our operations are expanding and the truth is that one of our greatest strengths is also one of our greatest weaknesses. As you know, we are very careful as to who we trust and as it is in all of society, we tend to feel more comfortable with those most like us. Therefore, many of our people will not trust those who come from different backgrounds or have different colored skin."

"You're looking for intelligence," I said.

"Yes. As we have grown, our ability to see around corners has not. Most of our people could never get jobs in law enforcement and therefore our access to real-time intelligence is limited. That is where you come into the picture."

"You're a moron," I said.

In a flash, Szymon had retrieved the shotgun and had it under my chin.

"Wait," Nekovar said, holding up a hand. He took another long pull from his cigarette.

To me he said, "I think that perhaps both you and my predecessor have underestimated your potential value."

"I'm not a cop anymore," I said.

He held up a finger as if I had arrived at an epiphany. "Exactly, Mr. Galloway. You see, we know you still have the ability to get information from your friends. Friends like Detective Chase Vinson, for instance."

I wasn't surprised they knew about my friendship with Chase, but I still tensed at the mention of his name.

"Too many men are shortsighted in this business," he continued. "Having a cop in your pocket can be valuable, but comes with risks. If it becomes evident that criminal elements are getting sensitive information regarding law enforcement, then the first people to come under scrutiny are those with direct access. However, if the individual you are controlling is one step removed from those who will be first suspected, then the trail will go cold if there is a search for the leak. It is wise to let the pawns take the risks and hold back the power pieces until absolutely necessary. Most in my organization believe I should simply kill you and be done with this business. However, I have decided to find out if you can be of any use to us. I don't think you are a pawn to be sacrificed. It is my hope that you may be a rook or a bishop, Mr. Galloway. But if it turns out you cannot benefit us, then you will be eliminated."

Szymon removed the barrel of the shotgun from under my chin and took a step back. Lying on my back on the kitchen floor, I was hardly a threat.

"You know I won't do it," I said. "You might as well tell the knucklehead over there to pull the trigger."

The old man smiled. "I know you have endured much at the hands of my associates. Now that I have met you in person, I can tell you are a man who does not fear your own death. Even the prospect of your impending demise does not seem to infuriate you. But, the federal agent who left here a few hours ago may value her life more."

I stopped breathing.

"Special Agent Jackie Fontree is still young," he said. "She could have a full life, and perhaps that life could be with you."

I sat up. Out of the corner of my eye, I saw Szymon toke a step forward.

"Yes," said Nekovar, blowing smoke in my direction. "You may not fear your own death, but you are able to fear the death of another."

Half a minute passed and nobody spoke.

"Do you know the Koliba Club?"

I told him I was familiar with the bar.

"I have established a place of business in the back room. In two days, you will come see me and you will provide me with the names and current aliases of two undercover narcotics officers. One of these individuals has befriended some of my associates who are often found at Trifecta Motorcycles.

The other undercover officer is working at one of our restaurants in East Liberty. We know the real identity of one of these people, so I will be able to verify the accuracy of the information you provide. If you fail to come see me at Koliba by midnight on the second day, Special Agent Fontree will be raped and killed. If you provide information that is untrue, Special Agent Fontree will be raped and killed. If you discuss our conversation with anyone, Special Agent Fontree will be raped and killed. If it comes to that, I will allow you to live long enough to fully experience the loss and then you will be tortured and eventually executed. I trust I have been clear."

He took a pull from his cigarette.

"You have two days before I act," Nekovar said. Then he grinned and added, "Unless I change my mind and decide it would be more motivating for you to suffer a loss before the deadline."

I started to speak, but then I caught a glimpse of the butt end of a shotgun coming toward the side of my head. Whatever else I had intended to say would have to wait until I woke in a few hours.

TRACK 10
"AN EARLY WAKE-UP FALL"

Somewhere in the distance, I heard a guitar riff. Although I was drifting in darkness, Jimmy Spartan's "Lukewarm Legacy" echoed throughout the recesses of my mind. It was a hit from Jimmy's third album which had been released in 1989, a period in which he like so many other musicians, was doing his best to shed the *glam* look that had become a sad cliché by the end of the decade. He'd cut his hair and ditched the leather pants in an effort to show growth and to capitalize on the grunge movement. The sound of that album had been a departure from Jimmy's previous work as well. He had forgone many of the studio tricks that many musicians used and was not afraid to leave in the small imperfections that made performances authentic. Although none of the songs on that album had been recorded live, listeners would hear the occasional pick scratch against a guitar string, or the unintentional rim of a drum being tapped underneath the powerful vocals. Every error was its own beautiful pen stroke on what some believed was Jimmy's signature accomplishment.

The main chorus became distorted by a shrill noise that, even with the recording's imperfections, seemed incongruous. Slowly my eyes opened and I was able to focus on a ladybug crawling across the ceiling of my kitchen. Jimmy's song faded completely, but the shrill sound repeated several more times before stopping. I sat up and rubbed my head, newly surprised at the lack of hair. My bandage, which was matted with blood, had been knocked off and was lying on the floor.

I managed to rise and the sound started up again. Now I recognized the ring tone, walked to my bedroom, and found my phone. I pressed an icon to accept the call from Chase.

"Yeah."

Chase chuckled. "Did I wake you?"

I reached down and turned the clock on my bed stand so I could read the display. It was only seven in the morning.

"Yeah," I said again, deciding it was appropriately early for my grogginess. I wondered if somehow Nekovar was listening. I was probably being paranoid, but it's not paranoia if people are really beating the hell out of you in your own house.

"I wanted to get you up to speed with the search," he said.

I reached up and touched my un-bandaged wound on my head. I brought my hand down and examined my fingers. No blood. The visit from Nekovar seemed like a dream, but I knew it wasn't.

"Trevor? Are you there?"

"Yeah. What girl?"

"Stretch's girlfriend, Keri Wilk. I was trying to track her down, remember?"

Chase's voice grew concerned. "Hey, are you straight? You didn't shoot up or anything, did you?"

I sat on the edge of my bed. "No. I'm straight. I was just up late." Then, in an effort to put his mind at ease, I added, "Jackie was here last night."

"Ah," he exclaimed. "It's fun being back in the saddle, but you may need some training wheels for a while."

"That makes zero sense," I said.

He laughed and said, "Anyway, our girl is in the wind and she's definitely in trouble. She has an apartment in Lawrenceville but someone beat me to it. It looks like somebody busted the lock and went through the place. From the looks of the closet and bathroom, she packed up and hit the road. She works at the Natural History Museum, but didn't show up for her shift and didn't call in sick. I'll spread the word that I'm looking for her, but she's not wanted and technically isn't a witness to anything. We don't really know if she's in danger, so I doubt I'm going to be able to get anyone to mobilize the troops on this one. I hate to say it, but she's on her own."

Although I knew I shouldn't have been feeling a great amount of concern for the girl who duped me, I wasn't ready to write her off.

"Do you think you can get someone to monitor her credit cards?" I asked.

"Dude," he said. "What do you think this is, an episode of *NCIS*? Would you like me to run the entire city through facial recognition while I'm at it?" he cracked.

I sighed. "I'm sure you still have contacts with the credit bureaus. What was that one girl's name? The one you said had a thing for cops and a talent for lap dancing?"

"Oh, you mean Michelle. I did like Michelle," he reminisced.

"Maybe it's time you two reunited," I suggested.

"Hmm. Maybe you're right. I do like to liaise with those in the financial business," he said. "In the meantime, I'll let you know if Wilk pops back up."

"Did Aymar run down the call Stretch made from his car?" I asked.

"Prepaid cell. He said he's going to see if the purchase can be traced, but you know how it will probably turn out if the phone was purchased with cash."

I did. Absent great security footage from wherever the phone was purchased, it was a dead end.

Chase's tone turned grave. "One more thing. The police chief in Monroeville is considering charging you."

"With?"

"Being unlicensed, disorderly conduct, discharging a firearm in a residential area, and probably some other violations."

"Why hasn't he?"

"Actually, it's a she, you sexist."

"Okay. Why hasn't she?"

"Aymar thinks she's waiting to see if you become a media darling who tried to save a boy and his mother, or a reckless lunatic who shot up a neighborhood."

"I guess it's a fine line," I said.

"The Monroeville chief called my chief to get background on you."

"Fabulous."

"Yeah. Needless to say, you need to go to ground for a while. Don't investigate shit. Even if Monroeville PD doesn't charge you, Pittsburgh might if you happen to bring any more attention to yourself. You can't afford any missteps."

"Thanks for the heads-up."

"Yup. Well, that's all I've got for now," said Chase.

I wanted to tell him about my visitors, but stopped myself. Nekovar knew a lot about me, Jackie and Chase. It wasn't inconceivable that my house was bugged, or that he had informants in the department. If I made one slip, one or both of them could get hurt.

"Okay," I said. "I'd appreciate any updates."

We ended the call and I sat there wondering what step to take next. It turned out I needn't have wondered, because someone else was about to take a tentative step toward me.

* * *

After showering and getting dressed, I took my phone into the backyard and dialed Jackie. I hoped she was still awake after a night of watching one of Planetary Electronics' new questionable "employees." I walked far enough from the house that there was no chance any listening devices would pick up the conversation. To any of my neighbors, I was just the average beaten-up man with a gunshot wound to the head, standing in his cold backyard to talk on the phone in the early morning hours. Nothing to see here, folks. Please move along.

"Hey you," Jackie answered.

"Did I wake you?"

"No, I just got home. We did a shift change before the target woke."

"Anything interesting happen?" I asked.

"Something is definitely about to happen. Before I started my shift, Joker rented a U-Haul box truck."

"Joker?"

"The guy I'm watching has a Joker tattoo on his forearm," she explained.

"Like from Batman?"

"No, the playing card."

"Cute," I said.

"Trust me, he's not," she said. "But, he's been a busy bee. My guess is these guys have a large shipment of record players stuffed with counterfeit coming in and are going to transport everything to Planetary Electrics to verify the contents before sending the U-Haul back out to various distribution points. If that happens, our agents can tail that truck and try to identify all of the major players in the distribution channel. Rather than have two or three people who can be compelled to provide information, we may end up with ten or twelve. It's possible we could effectively disrupt Peruvian counterfeit operations in this region and force the authorities in Peru to act."

"It sounds promising," I said, pulling my leather coat tighter around my body to combat the morning chill. "Look, I need to talk to you about something."

Nekovar had been explicit in his instructions regarding me keeping my mouth shut, but Jackie needed to know there had been a threat made against her. However, as I started to speak I irrationally started to wonder if it were possible my cell phone could be compromised. Nekovar's network was certainly powerful, but there was no way they had the ability to listen in on a cell conversation, right? Of course, I also had to consider that Jackie's house might be bugged and they could be listening in on her end of the conversation. If they even thought I had tipped her off though a phone conversation or in person, they might go after her. Hell, Nekovar had said he might go after her simply to make an example, but he had to know she was more valuable as leverage. I weighed my options and all of them weighed about ten tons and were cracking my spine.

"Be careful," I said. "Stay on your guard. Always."

"Of course," she said. "You too. Call me later and maybe we can get dinner before my shift tonight. Of course, if that box truck starts moving, all bets are off."

"Sounds good," I said.

We ended the call and I started thinking of any way I could secretly warn her of Nekovar's threat. Potential ideas were rolling around in my head like square marbles when I turned to find I wasn't alone in my yard. Not more than eight feet away from me, Keri Wilk stood shivering, and puffy-eyed.

"You have to help me," she sobbed.

"Are you okay? The police have been searching for you."

I took a step forward and she retreated like a frightened kitten.

I held up my hands and said, "I'm not going to hurt you, but I think you might be in some danger."

She nodded. "Some men came to my apartment and knocked the door down. I was able to get out the bedroom window, but I'm afraid to go back there."

"Let's go inside and talk," I suggested.

"No. Here is fine."

"Okay."

She wiped tears away and seemed to really look at me for the first time. I realized she was noticing all the bumps, bruises, and my nearly bare skull punctuated by the head wound.

"What on earth happened to you?"

I shrugged. "I'm not much of a people person."

"I'd say." She tried to smile, but the attempt melted from warm tears streaming down her face.

"How did you find me?"

"The internet," she replied.

"I'm not listed."

She looked at me as if I was the hopeless, credulous mark in a black and white detective flick. The dope who is being constantly bamboozled until a Bogart-like gumshoe reluctantly teaches him the harsh realities of a sinister world.

"It's the internet," she said. "Everyone is listed if you know where to look."

"Right."

She sniffed and used the sleeve of a tattered blue sweatshirt to wipe her face.

"They didn't say your name on the news, but was that you at Stretch's mom's house?"

"I was there."

"You shot the man who killed Stretch and his mom?"

I nodded. She took a deep breath and her nerves seemed to steady.

"He didn't kill Jimmy Spartan," she said.

"I know."

"You do? So, you know who killed him?"

"I have an idea," I said, realizing I did. "But, I'm not certain."

Keri asked, "Why did that man kill Stretch? He wasn't always straight with people, but he never hurt anybody." She paused and then said, "I should probably tell you that we were stealing from Jimmy. We took a lot of money—something like twenty-three thousand dollars. Maybe someone found out and that's why they went after Stretch and why someone is after me."

"Stretch told me about the theft, but didn't mention your role. You were in on it too?"

She nodded. "Mostly graphic design work for the clothing we were selling."

"Keri, Stretch told me that he might know who killed Jimmy. I think he may have called someone and tried to either warn or blackmail the person. Do you have any idea who he might have called? Did Stretch ever tell you he knew something about Jimmy's murder?"

"No. He never said a word and he would have if he had any idea who murdered Jimmy."

"How long were the two of you together?" I asked.

"Three years," she said.

Three years. You don't keep suspicions regarding a homicide from someone you've been with for three years. Keri was right. She faded from my focus and my vision blurred. My house and yard dissolved and the grass under my feet rolled back and exposed Stretch's hardwood floors. From a corner of the room, I could see Stretch standing across from...me, rubbing his throat. The conversation played out in front of me, the audio not quite synching with the video. Bits and pieces of the dialogue made it through and I did my best to fill in the blanks with my own memories of the conversation.

So, what had suddenly caused Stretch to think he knew who killed Jimmy? What in the world had cocked the pistol in his mind and clued him in on the identity of the killer? What was the variable that had ultimately led to Stretch and his mother being gunned down by an ice cold killer? Then, one small portion of the conversation between Stretch and me made it through and caused my created world to shatter into a million pieces, revealing Keri staring at me with apprehension and confusion.

It was me. It was all me.

I was the variable that got Stretch killed and now I knew which domino had been pushed.

It was all me.

"I need to call the police. They can keep you safe."

"No way. I just told you we were stealing from Jimmy. They'll put me away."

"That's not the priority right now. Whoever is after you must think Stretch told you something about Jimmy's murder. You have to go to the police."

She turned and started to leave.

"Wait," I said. "Do you have somewhere you can stay for a while? Somewhere you can lay low?"

"Not really."

"Do you have enough money for a hotel?"

"I have some credit cards."

"Wait here."

I went inside and returned quickly. I handed her some of the cash I had in the house.

"There is a Comfort Inn on Route 8 near Butler. Take this and get a room. Don't use your credit cards because I don't know who might be watching the transactions. You can give the desk a card for incidentals, but don't do anything that would cause them to run the card. No purchases and no calls from the hotel phone. Got it?"

She said she understood. I gave her my number and she programmed it into her phone.

"I'm going to go check on something and then I'll to come up there and we'll talk. We'll work this out."

She seemed reluctant, but capitulated. In reality, I was going to call Chase so both of us would show up at the hotel, but Keri didn't need to know that now.

She walked around the front of my house and I heard a car start. The humming of the engine faded and I went inside to make coffee. I was facing a major dilemma. Time was not on my side. Jimmy Spartan was going to stay dead, but Keri Wilk was very much alive and I wanted to keep her that way. I'd already gotten Stretch killed and Keri wasn't going to get added to the body count. I couldn't openly investigate anything, so that meant no formal police involvement. For Jackie's sake, I needed to keep my distance from her. Chase had already stuck his neck out for me more times than I could remember, so I needed to protect him if I could.

I felt I almost had a handle on the murder of Jimmy Spartan and the threat to Keri, but there was someone I needed to visit. With one conversation, I thought I could unravel the truth and protect Keri. But, that one conversation could crash an international investigation. No to mention, the person I needed to see inconveniently had a team of armed federal agents watching his every move.

Most of my memories of Tom Sonta were of him hauling a backpack of books through Planetary Electronics while giving a friendly smile to his father and whoever else happened to be present. Vince would ask Tommy how school had gone and the kid would politely remind his father that he preferred to go by Tom. Naturally, Vince would playfully tease the kid by saying things like, "Sure, Tommy. No problem, Tommy." He'd been a skinny, soft-spoken kid and I was sure he'd been bullied from time to time. I imagined assuming the shorter version of his first name was an attempt to shed his childhood and push his way into an adult existence in which he wouldn't have to deal with ridicule from those who were bigger or simply had more dominant personalities.

Now Tom was older, wore a full beard and was hobbled with a bad knee. From what Jackie had told me, he'd been getting pushed around by the new additions to Planetary Electronics landscape. Perhaps the added girth and facial hair had failed to conceal the temperament of the rail-thin kid who struggled to carry a heavy backpack.

Somehow, I needed to either get Vince's group to believe Keri didn't know anything or at least get myself some advance warning if they managed to get a line on her location. While I was hoping she would stay put in the hotel, she'd had a feral look in her eyes that I'd seen too many times before. She might remain stationary for a few hours, or maybe even a day, but her reliability had a short shelf life.

Going undetected while following Tom on his deliveries and conducting repairs was fairly easy. I'd arrived in Squirrel Hill at the same time as most of the workforce and managed to find a parking spot half a block away from Planetary Electronics and the Secret Service surveillance van. For two hours, I watched and waited as Vince and Tom arrived in a Toyota Camry. They turned down an unremarkable driveway that cut between two structures and led to the rear of their place of business. It was another hour until Tom pulled out in the same car. I watched as the Camry headed south down the hill and I waited for what I knew would follow. Sure enough, a silver Chevy Malibu carrying two men with short hair pulled out of a lot down the street and fell in behind Tom.

I wasn't overly concerned with being spotted by the pair of Secret Service agents. One rarely notices being watched while being immersed in the role of watcher. As long as I kept a few cover vehicles in between me and the Secret Service car, I'd be fine. I knew I didn't have to actually follow Tom, but could follow the agents instead. All of us were going to the same place—wherever that may be.

His first three stops were in pleasant residential areas filled with high-end foreign cars and yard art several steps above the common garden gnome. While under the watchful eye of the U.S. Secret Service, Tom approached the homes with nothing more than a tool box and left each of them within an hour. When Tom drove across town and pulled in front of another house, I started to think I'd never get the opportunity to speak with him in private. Then he limped past a cluster of private residences and hauled his tool box through the front door of a pizzeria marked by a giant sign with a smiling cartoon giraffe. I'd seen the commercials and knew it was primarily a place for parents to bring their kids who would devour mediocre pizza while running between video games.

I watched as the Secret Service found a spot down the street, then I drove around the block and parked on a parallel stretch. The tide of lunchtime traffic had been flowing in and out of the pizzeria when I'd driven past, so I thought I probably could have slipped in through the front without the agents keying in on me. They were watching Tom, not me, and shouldn't have had any reason to notice me. In fact, unless one of the agents had happened to have been in the area when Jackie and her partner Nick had saved my

ass, there shouldn't have been any reason for them to recognize me. To be on the safe side, I decided not to test my
theory of anonymity and opted to be slightly more covert.

I popped the trunk of the Jetta and dug around until I
found the socket set I'd put in there long ago. Without a
bandage on my head, my baseball cap now fit and I pulled
it low while walking to an alley behind the restaurant.
Doing my best to appear as if I was there for entirely legitimate reasons, I strode to the back door with confidence. I
gave the door a tug and found it was locked. Three hard
fist pounds later, the door opened.

"Yeah?" said a guy whose burly forearms projected out
from each side of a sauce-covered apron. He wasn't young
and struck me as the owner-manager type who would have
disposition that would never be mistaken for flowery.

"I'm with Planetary Electronics. Tom asked me to bring
him some tools he left behind."

He grunted and pointed a thumb behind him. I took a
step inside and he said, "Why didn't you just come through
the front like everybody else."

"I'm coming from another job a few blocks away. I
walked over so I didn't have to fight for a parking spot."

"Is that what happened to your face? Fighting for parking spots?"

"Oh, this? Nah. Had a little too much whiskey and took
a tumble. You know how it is."

"I'm a wine drinker," he said. I nodded as if I understood, although from his build and personality, I never
would have guessed. I really wanted to get to Tom, say my
piece, and get the hell out of there, but now Mr. Chatterbox the pizza guy wanted to commiserate with me.

"I used the hit the hard stuff when I was younger, but I
found that I felt classier when I drank wine. Since I felt
classier, I didn't feel like getting tanked. It's like some sort

of mental thing. You ever consider switching?"

I tried not to show my impatience and stayed jovial. "Yeah, but my problem is that I was told you are supposed to let the wine breathe."

"So?" he asked.

"Well I'd listen carefully, but never hear any sounds coming from the bottle. So I always ended up running over to give it mouth-to-mouth."

He enjoyed that and laughed much louder than I liked, but he gave me a pat on the back and showed me down the hallway. "Tom's in the dining area fixing the jukebox."

I thanked Mr. Chatterbox and moved down the hall until I got close to the main room. I peered around a corner to see if the agents would be able to see me through the giant plate glass window along the street. I thought I was hidden, so I leaned forward until I spotted Tom who was in a back corner kneeling next to neon-lit jukebox. He seemed to be concealed from the agents' position as well so I dipped my head to keep my face behind the bill of my cap and made my approach.

I kneeled down beside Tom and said, "Tom, we need to talk."

He did a double take. "Detective Galloway? What happened to you? Are you okay?"

"Keep working on that jukebox and act as if I'm helping you."

He looked down at the item in my hands and screwed up his face. "Why would I need a socket set?"

"Forget that," I said. "Just turn back toward the jukebox and listen."

He shrugged a shoulder. "Whatever you say, Detective."

"It's just Trevor," I corrected. "Tom, I know your dad has gotten in over his head with the wrong people. I have no idea what he's into," I lied. "But, I think Vince believes there is a girl out there that has information that could hurt him. The thing is, I've talked to her and she doesn't know anything. However, I think your dad sent some people to hurt her."

I braced myself for the inevitable argument that would be peppered with claims that his father could never have done such a thing and that I was off my rocker. I readied myself for the volley, but it never came. Instead, Tom's shoulders sagged and I thought he might somehow slip his entire body inside the machine he was repairing. There was a chance one of the agents would come inside to get a quick confirmation that Tom was still here. I didn't want this to take too long, but I waited him out.

"He was desperate," said Tom, almost inaudibly. "Money got tight and he was on the brink of losing the shop. Now the people he's been doing business with sent in some guys from Philly and Dad's scared."

This is where I had to create some distance as to not jeopardize the Secret Service investigation.

"Tom, I don't care about any of that. I'm not a cop anymore and I don't want to know what your dad got himself into."

"Then what do you want?"

"I simply want to keep the girl safe." I slid him a piece of paper on which I'd written my phone number. "If you hear anything about your dad or any of the new hired help getting a bead on the girl, let me know."

"What's her name?" he asked.

"It doesn't matter. If you pick up on them going after anyone, call me. Can you do that for me?"

"Yeah. I can do that. You really don't want know what my dad is into?"

I shook my head. "I really don't. I think I did enough damage to your family when I put your uncle away."

"You were good at it, you know."

I asked what he meant.

"Lying. You had us all fooled when you were doing undercover work. In fact, I started to call you Sean when you came up to me just now. But, I guess you aren't Sean Watkins anymore."

"I never really was," I said, patting him on the shoulder.

I got up and walked back across the dining area. Instinctively, I checked my surroundings and looked toward the plate glass window. An athletically built man with short hair walked past the window and glanced inside the pizzeria. I couldn't be certain, but I had a hunch it was one of the Secret Service agents trying to take a peek inside to confirm Tom hadn't snuck out the back. Whoever he was, he looked right at me and our eyes met. I continued on my path, made a turn down the hallway, and exited through the back door.

Would the agent have thought I was anything other than a customer or perhaps an employee? Was it possible that after my previous visit to Planetary Electronics, all of the agents had been given a copy of my photo and told to keep an eye out for me? Even if they had, with my new look I doubt I would be recognized. But still—was it possible that the agent would recognize me and then I would have to deal with being followed?

Get out of your head, Trevor. I was taking paranoia to a whole new level. If I became a surveillance target, Jackie would let me know. My watch said it was nearly two o'clock. She'd still be asleep for an hour or so. Then, I'd have to decide if I was going to try to tell her about Nekovar's threat or if she were safer without knowing. For now, I would drive to Butler and check on Keri Wilk. If nothing else, I honestly could tell her I'd made some headway into keeping her safe. If Tom had any knowledge

177

about Vince sending people after Keri, then I'd planted the seed that she didn't know anything and that chasing her around was futile. If he didn't know anything about Keri, then he would alert me if Vince and his thugs decided to make a move on her.

The drive to the Comfort Inn took me about forty-five minutes. On the way I popped a CD in the player and listened to some of Jimmy Spartan's fourth album, *Under the Fountain.* The album had a more mature feel to it than his previous works. The screech of candy apple red B.C. Rich guitars had been largely replaced by blues-influenced compilations ringing out from earth toned Gibson Les Paul six strings. Jimmy had made a leap with his lyrics as well, as there were fewer songs focusing on cocaine and strippers and more about heartache and desire. The album hadn't been as successful commercially as had his first records, but it did get a Grammy nomination for best album. It lost to an album made by a band that was publically humiliated the next year when a technical glitch during a live show revealed the band members were lip synching. That band broke up shortly thereafter while Jimmy kept his train headed down the tracks. He stayed the course as the careers of pretenders rose and fell, marking the heartbeat of an industry that had realized the illusion of quality could be manufactured with studio parlor tricks.

From the lack of cars in the parking lot, it appeared the Comfort Inn was nearly empty. I'd never seen what Keri had been driving, so I didn't know which one was her car, but I guessed it was a Subaru that had a "Coexist" bumper sticker that utilized symbols from various religions in spelling out the word. I entered the lobby and went to the front desk, knowing the routine.

"I'm here to see Keri Wilk, but I don't have the room number."

The obese man's nametag read, "Lewis M." He said, "I can't give you the room number."

Apparently, *he* didn't know the routine.

"Can you call her room and ask if it's okay to let me know the room number. Tell her Trevor Galloway is here to see her."

He blinked and said, "You can call her from the house phone. It's on that table by the elevators."

I watched him to see if he recognized the conundrum. He didn't.

"How can I call her if I don't have the room number?" I asked.

"You can pick up the phone, dial '0,' and this phone here will ring," he explained while pointing to the phone on the desk in front of him.

"And then you will connect me to her room?"

He thought this through.

"Yes."

"Fine."

I walked over to the table and picked up the house phone which was twenty feet away from Lewis M. I dialed "0" while looking at Lewis. "It seems to me this may not be the most efficient process," I remarked.

He picked up his ringing phone and said, "Thank you for calling the Comfort Inn. Please hold." He pushed a button on the phone, lowered the phone from his face, and said to me, "What do you mean?"

I rubbed my chin and said, "Lewis."

"Yes."

"You have me on hold."

Enlightenment crept around to where he was standing and he said, "Oh, sorry."

He pressed a button, taking me off hold and said, "What name is the room under?"

"Wilk," I said. "Keri Wilk."

He shifted over to a computer and spent way too long tapping on a keyboard. To stay calm, I counted tiles on the floor until he spoke again.

"Sir, we don't have anyone here by that name."

I was across the lobby instantly. "What do you mean? Check again."

He put the phone back in the cradle, looked at the monitor on the desk and said, "I'm sorry. When did she check in?"

"This morning."

He said, "Then, I'm afraid there has been some kind of mistake. I've been here all day and nobody has checked in during my shift."

I put my hands on the counter that separated me from Lewis. I knocked on the smooth surface while my thoughts raced. I didn't think Keri had been taken. She was a runner. I knew it when I'd looked in her eyes and I'd still chanced that she was scared enough to listen to reason. I'd been foolish to think she'd do what I asked and she was foolish for not taking my advice.

"Sir?"

I looked at Lewis who was eyeing my fist knocking on the counter.

"Sir," he began. "Maybe she'll check in later. If you leave me your name, I can let her know you stopped by. What's your name?"

I was barely listening and I felt as if my feet were enclosed in cement. Another mistake. I'd made another damn mistake. Is that what Lukas Derela had been trying to tell me from the backseat of my car? Was that the warning my dreamed-up version of Jimmy Spartan had been giving to me as he dangled from the Bridge of Sighs? Were my mental hauntings becoming clairvoyant?

"Sir?"

"Yes," I said, noticing he had a pen and paper in his hands. "I'm sorry. What did you say?"

"I asked who you are, sir."

I slid my hands off the counter and put them into the pockets of my jacket.

"I'm not entirely sure anymore," I said, walking out.

TRACK 11
"ONE LAST SHOVE"

Hoping the call would go to voicemail so I didn't wake her, I called Jackie. She didn't answer, so I left a message asking her to call me as soon as she got moving. I took the long way home, thinking of everything that had transpired over the past few days. If I had known that Traci Bermindo's request for me to follow up with her brother's death would have led to this, I would have walked away. I couldn't blame her for seeking closure, but I did blame her for putting a period at the end of our agreement by putting a bullet into her own head. What she had hired me to do was more complicated than a murder investigation. She wanted the truth to be known, but also to remain hidden. She wanted the world to know who killed Jimmy Spartan, but for his diagnosis of early Alzheimer's and the existence of a potentially disastrous final record to remain secret. And where the hell was that record, anyway? To my knowledge, it had yet to surface unless...

I changed course and drove to Stretch's apartment. With any luck, there wouldn't be any cops going through his place and I could do a systematic sweep. Perhaps Stretch had kept the record with hopes of putting it on the market to the highest bidder. The final, unreleased Jimmy Spartan album would be worth something regardless of the quality of the music. It was possible Stretch had taken it from Jimmy's and stashed it away somewhere. The recovery of the album wasn't my highest priority, but since I was currently being squeezed between the cops, a drug gang, and possibly a Peruvian-based counterfeiting operation, looking for piece-of-junk circle made of vinyl seemed a better idea than heading home to twiddle my thumbs.

I only had to wait a few minutes before I was able to piggyback off a FedEx delivery guy to gain access to Stretch's building. Once I made it to his door, I found it unlocked. The afternoon sun formed distorted squares across the wooden floors and dust particles floated through beams of warmth. Thanks to my years of narcotics work, I knew if there was anything I was good at, it was finding things that people wanted to remain hidden. I decided to start with the smaller rooms and then take on the large living room. Relief flowed through me as I realized Stretch hadn't been much of a reader and I wouldn't have to spend a great deal of time going through the bookshelves that were large enough to hide an album.

Forty-five minutes later, I had made it back to the living room and was down on one knee checking under the cushions of the sofa when something sent ice down my spine and electricity into my fingertips. Behind me, I heard the slow rhythmic sound of someone clicking their tongue against the roof of his mouth and then reshaping the mouth to alter the pitch. The resulting effect was noise similar to a water dripping, or...a ticking clock.

I knew without having to turn. "Get out of here, Derela."

The ticking continued. Reluctantly, I pivoted on my knee. He sat in a chair with his legs crossed and watched me intently while his mouth clicked off the seconds. If there was anything positive about my hallucination of Lukas

Derela, it was that he wasn't a particularly chatty soul. He really got my attention when he began chanting.

An angel on one shoulder, a devil on the other.
It is a matter of time until you take the life of another.

An angel on one shoulder, a devil on the other.
It is a matter of time until you take the life of another.

I pulled a folding knife out of my pocket and whipped it open. "Unless you're talking about the life of this couch, then you are wasting your breath," I said.

Plunging the knife into the material below one of the cushions, I continued. "You hid a lot of contraband in your day, Lukas. Where would you hide a record?"

An angel on one shoulder, a devil on the other.
It is a matter of time until you take the life of another.

An angel on one shoulder, a devil on the other.
It is a matter of time until you take the life of another.

Ignoring him, I used the knife to rip the material. I reached in and found nothing but a thin layer of foam and the framework.

"It's not here," I said to myself and probably to Drerela. "If Stretch took it, he didn't keep it here. He could have given it to Keri, but I think she was scared enough that she would have mentioned it. She was looking to distance herself from trouble in any way possible."

An angel on one shoulder, a devil on the other.
It is a matter of time until you take the life of another.

An angel on one shoulder, a devil on the other.
It is a matter of time until you take the life of another.

"Shut up, you ghoul," I said.
He did, and I turned to find the apartment empty.

On the drive home, I left another message for Jackie and flirted with the idea of calling Chase. I was still deliberating the merits versus the risks of making the call when I turned down my street. The decision had been made for me because Chase was standing in front of my house talking to two men I recognized as the detectives from the hospital. I pulled up to the curb and got out. Chase broke away from detectives Kent and Willis met me as I opened the car door. I figured one of three things had happened. Either the Monroeville PD or the Pittsburgh PD had decided to file criminal charges against me. It would be a hassle, but operating as a PI without a license was a misdemeanor and I could handle that kind of heat. The second possibility was Keri Wilk had been picked up by the cops and the detectives were making a house call to hear me explain how and why I had tried to stash her away in a hotel. The third, and by far the worst, possibility was that the department had been watching Stretch's apartment and I was about to be charged with breaking and entering and a myriad of other crimes that could carry real jail time. Judging from Chase's expression and the presence of the other detectives, I was about to be the recipient of a little quiet time in a locked room.

I got out of the car and stood in the open door. "Chase," I said. "What are you doing here?"

In all the years I'd known Chase Vinson, he'd never been at a loss for words. Now we stood facing each other with the October sun dipping beneath the distant horizon, and he seemed to be searching desperately for any scrap of a syllable.

"Trevor, I have some bad news."

Dammit. It was Keri. Whoever had been on her trail had caught up to her. I should have stayed with her. I should have thrown caution to the wind and called Chase immediately. I should have done…something.

"It's Jackie," he said. "She's gone."

My world ended.

All of my worlds ended.

"A neighbor called it in after hearing people yelling from inside her house. By the time units got there, it was too late."

I dropped back into the seat of my car, with my feet flat on the cold street.

"How?" I said.

"There will be time for that la—"

"How?" I repeated.

"It looks like someone tried to strangle her in her bedroom. She put up a fight. I'm told that from the way her knuckles and fingernails looked, she did some damage to her attacker. In the end, she was stabbed."

The sun sank a little further and the shadows reached out to me.

"I'm sorry, Trevor. I'm so sorry."

I lowered my head, stared at the ground, and felt sick. Those bastards. Those inhuman bastards.

"Why are they here?" I asked, referring to the other detectives.

"They caught the case and remembered Jackie was with you at the hospital. They just want to ask you some questions about her associates and fill in the timeline. You know how it works. We can go inside and talk."

I did know how it worked. I understood how all of it worked.

"Can you tell them to give me a minute?" I asked. "I need a minute."

"Yeah. Of course," he said and then he walked away.

My eyes filled with tears and my chest felt like it was imploding. I doubled over and fought back the vomit. Sitting up to catch my breath, I wiped my eyes, turned and saw Chase explaining things to the detectives who appeared to be sympathetic. In the background, I saw movement in my living room window. Only the blurred form of person was visible, but I knew who was there. I knew the form was beckoning me to capitulate to the circumstances, and walk inside with the detectives so I could begin sorting through the fucking stages of grief. What good would that do? More time wasted on a life now devoid of any hope or meaning.

I ignored the person in the window and once again my eyes found the street between my feet. My eyes blurred and the portrait around me smeared into a colorless quicksand, but this time I didn't find myself bearing witness to someone else's past crime. This time I saw my future. Reality re-emerged, but the street in front of me glowed crimson.

How about I save everyone some time and skip ahead through the stages of grief? I thought.

I had no use for denial. Not a single fucking use.

I'd found anger.

I knew anger.

I didn't check my rearview mirror once as I sped away.

In the twenty years the Koliba Club had been in business, not one honest person had stopped there for a beer and a shot. However, I wasn't going to walk through the front door with guns blazing, since doing so would probably keep me from my objective. Besides, I had no guns to blaze.

I circled the block and saw what I needed to see. I

parked the Jetta near the east end of the alley that ran behind the club, but pulled forward far enough that the sentry
I'd seen guarding the back door wouldn't spot the car. Then,
I took a walk around the block to the south, staying out of
sight of the club and the alley. When I arrived at the west
end of the alley, opposite my car, I waited for the man to
turn his attention to the east during his periodic visual scans.

His head swiveled and I made my approach. When I was
twenty feet from him, his head had started to turn my direction, but with my left hand in my pocket, I pressed the
panic button on my key fob. The sound of my car alarm
brought his attention back to the east until I was within
five feet of his position. Sensing my presence, he spun and
reached under his windbreaker. With my right hand, I
plunged my folding knife deep under his chin. Both of his
hands grabbed my wrist, but it was too late. I withdrew my
left hand from my pocket and pushed his head back into a
brick wall while covering his mouth and nose. He struggled
longer than I expected, but eventually stopped breathing
and I let him slide down the wall. I folded the knife, put it
away, and reached into the dead man's jacket withdrawing
the semi-automatic pistol he'd wanted. Then I found my
keys and silenced the car alarm. I slid his body behind a
dumpster and tossed some tattered garbage bags on top of
it. I returned to the back door and checked the gun in my
hand. The metal handle of the door relinquished its chill as
I pulled.

A red-orange EXIT sign lit the path in front of me. A
closed door at the end of the hallway appeared to separate
the semi-legal business of the bar from the elicit business of
the back rooms. Music boomed from the bar area and the
sounds heavy beats covered my approach. One door was
on the right and another was farther away, on the left. I
moved forward quickly and had nearly reached the room

on the right when a man in a red T-shirt came out of the door. He spotted me, saw the gun in my hand, assessed my intent, reached behind his back and began to yell. I hit him in the temple with the butt of the pistol and he staggered. He regained his balance and lurched forward, surprising me with his quickness and managed to knock the pistol out of my hand as we fell to the floor. We both scrambled to our feet and Red Shirt managed to pull the knife he had behind his back. He attacked, but his technique was off-balance and clumsy. He lunged at my abdomen and I shifted my position and moved left, off-line of the attempt. His momentum carried him wildly as he stabbed nothing but air, allowing me to use the thumb of my right hand as a weapon to gouge out his right eye with a ferocious jab. He dropped to his knees and wailed in pain while bringing his hands up to protect his face. I located the pistol, and having lost the element of surprise anyway, fired a shot into his head.

As Red Shirt fell, a bullet whizzed past me. I looked up and saw a handgun pulling back from the same doorway Red Shirt had come out of. On the floor, I saw a trace of a shadow creeping out from where the individual had retreated, telling me my adversary was still taking shelter behind the corner of the doorway. I glanced at the walls. Simple drywall. Something important you learn in law enforcement is that there is a huge difference between cover and concealment. The engine block of a pickup truck is cover. Cheap drywall is concealment. I took aim at the drywall next to the doorframe and fired three rounds. A skinny man's body slumped forward and sprawled into the hallway.

I stepped over Mr. Skinny and swung into the doorway on the right. I found nothing but a series of connected supply rooms and no other threats. The shots I fired would have been audible over the music, so I raced to the door leading to the bar and found it had a rudimentary lock. I turned the lock and then went back to get Red Shirt's bulky body. I managed to pull the body to the end of the hall and prop the dead weight against the door.

Next, I headed to the only other door in the hallway, which had to have been an office. My initial instinct was to rush through the door and obliterate everything. However, I remembered who might be in there and that they heard me coming, I stopped. I stood to the side of the door and put my back against the wall.

With my right hand, I used the gun to pound twice on the door while I shouted, "Nekovar!" before ducking out of the way.

A shotgun blast sounded and pellets perforated the center of the door. As I heard the shooter rack the weapon to chamber another shell, I burst through the door and aimed at the first thing I saw. I fired three rounds center mass into Szymon. The tough bastard stayed on his feet and pointed the gun in my direction as I put another two rounds into him. He dropped the weapon and fell hard, revealing a man sitting at a round wooden table in the center of the room. On the table sat a bottle of vodka and a glass. He eyed me warily as he poured a drink. I approached with my gun at the ready until I stood across the table from the old man. He slid the glass across the table.

"You are early," he said.

"Did you kill Jackie?" I asked. The simple mention of her name sent a million powerful emotions through my body.

His expression was unreadable. I might as well have asked him his opinion of the Periodic Table.

"You mean you do not know?" he asked. "You walk in here, kill my men, and you are not certain of your cause?"

"Did you?" I asked.

"I did not," he said with a smirk. It was not a smirk of

self-assurance or righteousness. It was the smirk one sees when confronting a survivor. It was the sneer the devil shows you before he swallows you whole.

I reached down, grabbed the glass with my free hand, and downed the drink in one gulp.

He must have seen something behind my eyes because he said, "Even if you do not believe me, you do not know for sure that I have done this thing."

I placed the glass back on the table and said, "You're right. I can't know for sure." Then, I leveled the gun at his head.

His manner changed from one of smugness to one of outrage.

"You know who I represent," he snapped. "You know what will come down on you if any harm comes to me! Who do you think you are?"

My eyes locked on his. He asked the question, so I gave him the answer.

"I'm the Tin Man."

He leaned back and blood drained from his face. He opened his mouth to say something else, so I put a bullet into it. His head lurched back and he looked to Heaven as his soul descended to Hell. While life gurgled from Pavel Nekovar, I poured myself another drink.

I needed one for the road.

TRACK 12
"FIGHT TO THE BREATH"

The wind picked up as any suggestion of the sun was erased from the sky. The bustling traffic along Murray Avenue produced its own blanket of sound and the headlights and taillights of the cars shuffled up and down a few feet at a time. I parked the car several blocks away from my destination, grabbed my baseball hat from the passenger seat, and slipped it over my head. With the surveillance van parked nearby, I wanted to be as covert as possible. It wasn't that I cared about getting caught. I cared about getting stopped.

With the Secret Service operation ramping up, and with the agents being extra vigilant after losing one of their own, the worst thing I could have done would be to make an attempt to sneak around and hop a few fences to stay out of sight. The business should have been closing, so walking through the front door could have resulted in me pushing on a locked door while federal agents took photographs. Besides, I wanted to see what Vince had going on behind the scenes as opposed to the limited view customers got across from a glass counter. I knew if I simply walked up to the store and cut through the narrow driveway that led to the rear entrances of a couple of the businesses, I'd just be another guy minding his own business in a beehive of economic activity.

I still had four bullets in the gun I'd taken from the sentry at the Koliba Club and in my fluctuating between rage and numbness, I hadn't thought to take another gun off any of the men I'd dropped. It didn't matter. One way or another I was going to end anyone I thought might have been responsible for Jackie's murder. I let gravity pull me down the hill as I walked along the sidewalk opposite the van parked on the left side of the street. Keeping my hat low and my head turned a few degrees to the right, I made it to the driveway and between the two buildings before turning toward the rear entrance of Planetary Electronics. I couldn't see much of the rear entrance because there was a U-Haul box truck backed up to a loading dock. It was the same type of truck Jackie had told me the man with the joker tattoo had rented, presumably to pick up and distribute a shipment of record players and turntables loaded with counterfeit currency.

I hopped up onto the dock and saw the roll-up door at the rear of the truck was open. I peeked inside and saw crates stacked on top of each other, some secured in place by wide yellow cinch straps with metal buckles. From the state of disarray, it appeared the merchandise was in the process of being unloaded. Pulling out my phone to use it as a flashlight, I stepped inside the rear of the truck and used my free hand to pull out my knife. I pried open one of the crates, dug through packaging foam, and saw the top of a record player. After tucking the knife back into my pocket, I propped my phone against the interior of the truck as to keep the crate in the light. I wedged my hands between the wooden sides of the crate and the record player and pulled until it slid out. I kneeled down and put it on the floor of the truck, flipped it over, stood and stomped on the bottom until the casing cracked open exposing stacks of currency. I gripped the stacks in my hands and glared at them before letting them fall to the steel floor.

Paper and ink.

If Vince had been responsible in any way for Jackie's death, then she had been killed for nothing more than paper and ink. How could one justify ripping away a human being's existence over something that would be of no more value than a common street flyer if a government had not declared it to be of monetary value? How were these bills more important than a beating heart? They weren't more important. Not to me.

A door squeaked somewhere behind me and I snatched up my phone and killed the light. I moved closer to the front of the cargo area as the truck sunk and lifted as someone stepped inside. The outline of a man came into focus and I saw him feel around while letting his eyes adjust to the darkness. He shuffled forward until his foot struck the record player I'd left on the floor.

"What the—"

He drew a revolver and swept it from side to side as his eyes frantically searched for a target. Firing my own weapon would likely bring the Secret Service running around the building, so I waited until his gun traced an arch and passed my position before leaping forward and punching him squarely in the jaw. I heard the man's gun drop and hit a stack of crates while I delivered two more punches to the body. The man shoved me away to create some distance and delivered a solid side kick that hit me above the knee. If the kick had landed a few inches lower, it would have shattered my knee and left me vulnerable to an attack. I recovered my balance and reengaged the blond man who I could now see well enough to know I didn't recognize. Likely one of the new arrivals Jackie had told me about, in the process of unloading the shipment.

Blondie kept his fists up, but made the mistake of taking

his attention off of me as he let his eyes hunt for the dropped gun. I reached in my pocket for my knife, but Blondie caught the movement and charged forward, tackling me to the ground. He pinned me to the floor and landed a punch to my mouth before I was able to push him up a few inches, causing him to naturally oppose the action by letting his full weight fall on me. That's what I had wanted. As he fell into me, I launched my head off the floor, striking him in the nose with my forehead. He lurched back. I rolled him off of me and clawed my way onto his back as he tried to slink away.

I grabbed the hair on the back of his head and slammed his face into the floor twice before he managed to catch me with an elbow. He slid forward again and I saw why. His fingers were now on the dropped gun and he was establishing a grip. I managed to get one arm around his neck and my other hand on the gun. I contracted my left bicep and cut off his air supply while both of us maneuvered our right hands on the pistol, my hand on top of his. I got my thumb behind the hammer of the un-cocked revolver and I felt it struggle back as he pulled on the trigger. If he got a shot off, the echo from inside the truck would be substantial. It would only be seconds before I was surrounded by Vince's crew and only seconds after that we would all be taken down by federal agents.

Without easing up with my left arm, I summoned all the strength I could in my right thumb to keep the hammer from drawing back to where the gun could be fired. We stayed in this position for half a minute before I felt his grip on the gun ease. After half a minute more, there was no struggle at all. I sat up, caught my breath, and checked Blondie's pulse by putting my fingers on his neck. I felt nothing coming through his veins, but did start to feel something remorseful inside me. Then I thought of Jackie fighting for her last breaths. Then I picked up the revolver and grabbed one of the loose cinch straps that had been holding some of the crates in place before getting out of the truck to finish what I came to do.

The back entrance of Planetary Electronics led to the basement of the three-story building. If the crew was unloading the crates to check and possibly redistribute the counterfeit notes, they would do it in the basement rather than carry the boxes up multiple flights of stairs. That meant I was walking into ground zero to confront an unknown number of adversaries who were certainly armed and on-edge. *Screw it.*

I swung the door open and a stocky man in a tight black T-shirt and military-style BDUs was standing in the hallway while smoking a cigarette while reading off a clipboard. The man was leaning against a wall next to a mounted fire extinguisher and he didn't look up as I advanced toward him.

Assuming it was Blondie coming back in with a crate, he touched a pen to the papers on the clipboard and said, "This makes thirteen. Devon is coming down with the dolly and that will speed things up."

"Hey," I said, getting his attention.

I was holding the nylon cinch strap in my right hand and had the weighty metal buckle slung over my shoulder. When he turned his head in my direction, I swung the buckle at and it connected with a stony thud. The clipboard hit the ground a split-second before his bloodied head did the same.

A voice boomed from around a corner. "Everything okay out there?"

I headed toward the sound and watched as the front portion of a moving dolly rolled into view. The rest of the dolly swung into the hallway and I saw it had been converted into a four-wheeled cart with a long, flat vertical portion capable of carrying stacks of boxes. This meant using the cinch strap again would be more difficult since there was going to be several feet of separation between me and who-ever was pushing the cart in my direction.

I saw the man's arms first. To be more specific, I saw the man's right forearm. A tattoo of a playing card was stenciled on skin that was still holding a tan from the summer months. It was the man Jackie had been following the night before. The same man who had rented the truck that was now loaded with counterfeit money.

"Joker," I said involuntarily as he came around the corner and came face to face with me.

Actually, we weren't face to face since his face was at a different altitude than mine. I stopped and wondered at the muscular tower whose head was nearly scraping the ceiling. He came to a standstill, glowered at me, and then looked over me to see his comrade slumped on the floor. Joker's face tightened and his feelings about my presence became clear. My plan had involved stealth. My plan needed to change. I dropped the nylon strap and with both hands reached behind my back to pull the two pistols I was carry-ing. The cart slammed into my shins and I fell forward on-to it before I was even able to touch a pistol grip.

The cart rolled back through the hallway, spun around, and came to a stop near the man I'd hit with the strap. I tried to stand on my own to get into a defensive position, but hands were on me before I could get both feet planted on the floor. Joker had me against a wall and plunged a fist into my stomach. Then, he gripped the collar of my leather jacket, did a one hundred and eighty degree turn, and slammed me into the opposite wall. His hands slid from my jacket to my throat and he lifted me off the floor while squeezing my windpipe. I gripped his wrists and did what I could to force him to release me, but he was too strong.

That's when I noticed the details of his wrists and forearms.

There were fresh scratches and bruises everywhere along his arms, as if he had been in a battle with a lion—or a woman who would never back down in a fight. The scratches and bruises led up his biceps and disappeared under his shirt, only to reappear on his neck. Then, in a split second I realized what had happened.

Joker had spotted the tail and somehow had managed to turn the tables on Jackie and follow her home. With a large shipment coming into town, he had to find out what agency was onto them and how much they knew. He had tried to get the information out of her, but she didn't tell him anything or else they would have diverted the shipment or changed the schedule. She had fought to the end and this son of a bitch had ended her life. Regardless of whether he acted on his own or took orders from Vince, he didn't get to walk away from something like that. Whatever his part was in this operation, he was here because it was his job. I wasn't here for a job. I was here for a cause. When a man doing a job confronts a man with a cause, the smart money goes on the true believer.

I released his wrists and flattened my left hand on the side of his head while pressing the thumb of my right hand into the soft spot located under his left earlobe. The pressure point is called the mandibular angle and it doesn't work on everyone. It worked on Joker enough that his grip on my throat loosened enough that I was able to shift my hands down. I brought my palms back up under his arms, knocking them toward the ceiling and causing his grip to release. I slid down the wall and my feet hit the floor.

Taking advantage of my footing, I kneed him in the groin, and then landed three solid punches to his face. He staggered, but started to recover. On the wall next to me was the fire extinguisher I'd seen earlier. I ripped it off the wall and smashed the base into Joker's nose. He groaned, fell down, and covered his face, affording me the opportunity to draw the semi-automatic I'd taken from the Koliba Club. I stood over him, pointing the gun at his head. He looked up at me through the blood trickling down his face.

"You killed Jackie," I said.

He turned his head and spat blood. "The Fed?"

"Yeah," I said. "The Fed."

He didn't deny it. He didn't react at all.

"Are you a cop?" he asked.

I shook my head.

He was perplexed. "Then who the hell are you?"

He asked the question, so I gave him the answer.

The sound of shots emanating from the basement of a building in a business district may not have been enough to cause more than a few heads to turn out on the street. Most of the pedestrians on Murray Avenue probably shrugged off the pops as a distant car backfire, or someone hammering plywood over a broken window. If the Secret Service agents heard anything at all, they wouldn't know for sure if the shots had come from inside Planetary Electronics or some other location. I knew they wouldn't risk blowing the counterfeit operation because one or two agents *thought* the sound of gunfire came from the target location. However, the story was different inside the building. Once the shots rang out, I heard rapid footsteps.

I dropped the empty semi-automatic and drew the revolver. My ears rang from the shots I'd fired and my nostrils were filled with the scent of gunpowder. Turning the corner, I noticed the hallway transformed from one that had been finished with drywall and drop ceilings to one lined with wood slats, loose wires, and copper pipes. A flickering fluorescent light drew me forward and through a doorway.

The room in front of me was mostly empty, with the exception of some tall shelves in a corner and a few wooden crates sitting next to a toolkit on the cracked concrete floor. Some of the crates had been opened, the record players and turntables removed. One turntable appeared to have been carefully opened and counterfeit notes were stacked a short distance away.

A voice came from a darker portion of the room. "I can explain."

"You don't have to, Vince."

He was sitting behind a desk. His hands were on the dented metal surface and he didn't appear to be armed. The flickering lights reflected off his eyeglasses.

"It started small, but got out of hand. Nobody—"

"Was supposed to get hurt," I said, finishing his sentence. "They never are."

"Are you going to kill me?" he asked.

"Yes."

"I have valuable information. I know all about the people who bring in the money. I know where it's all going."

"It's paper," I said, taking a step in his direction. The silver revolver dangled at my side. "It's just paper."

He looked at the gun and then at my face. "Devon wasn't supposed to kill the girl. He went off on his own. The man is a psychopath. All of the guys they sent from Philly are sadists. They walked in and started throwing their weight around."

"They didn't kill Jimmy Spartan," I said. "They had nothing to do with him."

"Jimmy was—"

"A mistake. I know. This all started with a mistake," I said.

Lukas Derela had tried to tell me. Jimmy had told me in

my dream.

"You delivered the wrong turntable to Jimmy," I said. "Either your supplier had put counterfeit notes in the wrong device, or you delivered the wrong turntable. Maybe Jimmy discovered the counterfeit, or you simply tried to recover it without him knowing. The two of you argued, so you killed him and took the turntable. End of story."

"No," he said. "I could never kill anyone, Trevor. Not Jimmy and not you. I didn't even know that the Peruvians had sent that man to shoot you in your home."

"Roger Orta called you the day he was killed," I said, remembering Stretch's mysterious phone call. "What happened, Vince? How did he know you were involved with Jimmy's murder?"

Vince sighed. "Jimmy had tried to use the turntable, but it didn't work. He called here and wasn't happy about it. I couldn't ask him, but I was afraid he'd found the money inside, so I said I'd come out there the next day and explain everything. Sometime after that call, Jimmy had been recording at his house and Orta had admired the turntable. Jimmy made some off-hand remark about how I had some explaining to do, but let it drop. I guess when you said something to the kid about the missing turntable, he figured it out."

Something still didn't make sense to me.

"He called a prepaid cellphone," I said. "You said he called here."

Vince's expression saddened. "I've known Stretch since he was a kid and I've worked on his sound equipment. I don't use my cellphone often, so I just keep a pay-as-you-go cell."

"So you sent an assassin to take care of him."

"I told you. I couldn't kill anyone. It's not in me."

"That was a nice touch with the car by the way."

He tilted his head.

"I didn't put it together at first, but when the cops ran the VIN of the assassin's car, it didn't come back on file. I wondered how the man had acquired an unregistered car, but then I remembered you told me your brother is out on parole and working for a car dealership. I'm guessing that he let you borrow a car that couldn't be easily traced. Smart move."

"He didn't know what was going on," Vince explained. "He was only doing me a favor."

I raised the revolver and pointed it at Vince. He didn't flinch, just kept talking.

"That turntable was supposed to be clean and we didn't think to check it before giving it to Jimmy. None of this should have happened."

With one word reaching my ears, my body tensed and I knew what was coming.

We.

Vince had said *we.*

Something whipped around my neck and I was pulled backwards to the point my toes barely touched concrete. I raised the revolver and tried to point it behind me, but another hard yank caused it to fall from my hand. My fingers searched for any slack in whatever was constricting around my neck, but there was none to be found. My assailant was using some sort of electrical cord, I guessed.

My peripheral vision started to fade until all that was left in front of me was a tunnel circling around Vince. I looked in his face. He wasn't coming to help me, but he wasn't coming to help finish me either. He seemed to be frozen with indecision. Then the tunnel swirled faster and the rest of the pieces fell into place.

Vince had told me that Tom had helped him place the overseas orders. It was Tom who was responsible for deliveries. Jackie had told me that when Tom had been getting pushed around on the street in front of the surveillance van, Vince had been watching through the window. He had been unable to help his son because the Philly crew had moved in and taken the operation from Tom, not Vince. Tom had been the one who had tried to sneak into Jimmy's house to retrieve the turntable. Jimmy had surprised Tom and turned his back on the man he knew. It was Tom's mess and he had to clean it up. Vince wasn't running anything. Vince wasn't capable of murder. But, evidenced by the fact he was killing me, Tom was capable of anything. Tom had killed Jimmy, and now I would die at his hands as well.

The cord bit into my skin and my legs flailed helplessly. I knew from Tom's point of view, I couldn't be allowed to live. If I survived, he would either be killed by me or spend the rest of his life in prison. Everything would be taken from him. Everything.

I looked at Vince, who sat motionless. I tried to stare into his eyes, but my glare couldn't get through the reflection in his eyeglasses. I watched myself being strangled and then I saw the briefest of flashes in those lenses. Something metallic blazed at the bottom of the reflected image and I realized I had one chance. Whatever fury I had left inside began to erupt. These men could not be allowed to win. I wouldn't allow it.

There are two types of men you must fear in this world: Men who have everything to lose—and men like me.

I swung my legs up toward the ceiling and then brought both of my heels back toward Tom's knee brace. He made a sound and his knee gave, causing us both to collapse to the ground. Gasping for air and trying to regain my full vision, I felt around on the floor. Tom kicked me in the ribs and I rolled several times until I was on my back. I felt something solid against my spine and got one arm under me. Tom, dragging one leg, slid forward and raised his foot above my head, intending to stomp me unconscious. I brought the revolver around and fired five rounds into his chest.

"No!" Vince yelled as Tom stumbled back and then dropped to a sitting position.

Tom appeared to be in complete disbelief that he was mortal. But then his head drooped, and his breathing stopped. His body toppled over. It looked like he had simply fallen asleep, if not for the holes in his chest. Vince scurried to his son and cradled his head. He sobbed while I struggled to my feet and tried to regain my breath.

"Just kill me," he said.

I squeezed the .357 Smith & Wesson revolver tight. I'd fired five of the six rounds and all of them had been deafening. While the Secret Service agents may have been able to explain away the sounds of the first shots, five more from the same area were bound to draw some attention. I didn't care about getting caught, but I did want to go say goodbye to someone before I was taken into custody.

"Do it!" Vince yelled.

"No," I replied, surprising myself.

Jackie wanted to close her case and I had left one person who could help the government do that very thing.

"What?" he said through tears.

"You are at least partially responsible for Tom's death. You're going to have to live with that. Not to mention, you are about to be raided by federal agents and the Peruvians are going to be furious that you lost a shipment of this size. You'll be a liability to be eliminated at all costs. You can either give up everything you know and pray the Peruvians don't find you in witness protection, or you can get your throat slit in prison. Those are your options."

He wiped his eyes and said, "I could run."

I shot him in the leg and he screamed.

"Those are your options," I repeated.

He pressed down on the wound and writhed in pain. "You can't leave me alive. The police will ask me who came in here and shot the place up and I'll tell them it was you."

"I don't care," I said. "I really don't. But, I promise that if I see you again I'll hurt you more than you can imagine. Whether we happen to meet in a city park or in a penitentiary, I'll pile more pain on top of you than anything you can dream up. So, tell them whatever you want."

I turned to leave, but stopped and walked back to where Vince bled on the floor.

"Do you still have the record?" I asked.

"What?"

"There was a record in Jimmy's house and it's missing. Was it on the turntable Tom took after he killed Jimmy?"

"What does it matter?" he asked.

I stepped on the bullet hole in his leg.

"Yeah, there was a record," he screamed. "It's upstairs on a shelf under my workbench, along with a bunch of other worthless albums. What difference does it make?"

I found a set of stairs that led up to the main level and found Vince's shop. In the back room, a stack of records sat on a table and I thumbed through them. One was in a white sleeve and didn't have any markings. I slid the vinyl from the sleeve and read the label in the center of the black disk. The label had nothing on it more than the initials JS. Vince and Tom probably didn't even know what they'd had when they took the record off. They must have thought the album was simply one of Jimmy's previously released albums and was of no major significance. I put the vinyl back in the sleeve, leaving bloody fingerprints on the paper. I walked over to a phone, dialed nine-one-one, and said the words, "Shots fired," and gave the address. I left the phone off the hook, walked back down the stairs and out the back door.

EPILOGUE

"Will you be arrested?"

"Yes."

"Will you be convicted?"

"Probably," I said.

Dr. Welch didn't bother to take notes this time. This visit was more personal than professional. I'd walked in and put Jimmy's album on the record player in the corner. The music filled the room as we talked.

"You could plead temporary insanity," she suggested.

I sat in the middle of the couch and didn't say anything. She was right, of course. But, none of that seemed relevant at the moment.

She said, "I wish I could testify on your behalf."

"I know."

"You can say it was self-defense. The story can be that you went to talk to these men and they attacked you."

"All of them?" I said, rhetorically.

She looked at the floor, digging for more options but only finding land mines.

"It was a psychological break," she said. "You snapped and lost all control."

"Possibly," I replied.

I could feel the empathy rolling off of her. She was wishing she had been able to do something to stop me. In fact, she had tried.

She asked, "Will you have to stop seeing me for a while?"

"You know I will."

"Because you will be forced to take the pills?"

I nodded. "I assume."

"I shouldn't say this, but I'll miss these visits, Trevor."

"Me too," I replied as I let the music wrap around me.

Jimmy's final work was like nothing he'd done before. Knowing about his Alzheimer's, I could hear it was the story of a man who was desperately clinging to his reality, while attempting to accept a new one. There was sorrow, fear, and ire in his words and he had broken free from worrying about the opinions of others. With the impending loss of his faculties, he had found a sense of sovereignty within his own mind.

Headlights from the street walked across the wall and Dr. Welch said, "The police are here."

"Yes," I said as the volume of the music seemed to increase.

"I stood in the window and tried to get you to stay," she said.

"I know. I saw you."

"But you couldn't stay."

The music grew louder.

"What about the girl you were trying to help? Keri?"

"She's a survivor," I said. "She'll be fine."

Dr. Welch stood up and got out of her chair—my chair— and, as always, it failed to swivel one inch. She sat next to me on her couch—my couch—and we listened to the music. I glanced at the clock on the wall, the one I had owned for longer than I could remember. The second hand seemed to slow as if too exhausted to continue with the effort. From the direction of the kitchen, Lukas Derela walked in and sat on the other side of me. He looked at me and winked.

An angel on one shoulder, a devil on the other.

I'd left the front door ajar and Chase pushed it open. Hesitantly, he walked inside and saw me sitting on the couch. Alone. He came closer and spoke, but I couldn't hear the words. Only the music. The notes slid smoothly through my head. Detective Willis and Detective Kent entered the room and seemed content to let Chase do the talking. They leaned in close to each other and had a conversation while Chase continued talking to me. He gestured and tried to keep my attention while he studied the blood on my hands.

Then, more people filed into the room, although I was the only one to notice. They were people from my past who had no reason to be here. A fatality from a traffic accident I worked as a rookie. A classmate who had drowned when we were in the fourth grade. In walked a man who had committed suicide after his wife had left him. I had delivered the death notification to his family. Some of the other faces were familiar, but I had difficulty placing them. I saw an accountant I had not been able to save after he overdosed from a bad batch of heroin. The number of faces grew exponentially. Too many to recognize. Too many to answer to.

In the middle of the crowd, Chase was still talking. The music kept getting louder.

After getting kicked out of VMI, I'd finished my degree at the University of Akron. Now, a girl I'd met at the end of my junior year walked into my living room. At the end of the school year, we'd met at a party and had hit it off, but I'd failed to ask for her phone number. I never found out exactly what happened to her, but I remembered reading her obituary in the school paper when I returned from summer break. She was here. They all were here, filling the room like notes being penciled into sheet music. All of them were looking at me, some nodding acknowledgment, some eyes filled with animosity. Jackie walked in and smiled at me. I started to cry and my hands shook.

Before long, the room was filled with more people than I could count, but the detectives saw only me. Chase stepped back to give me space. The three cops huddled in the doorway, unsure what to do. Another song ended and Kent made a slight gesture that I should go with them. It was a kindhearted wave, rather than a command. I stood, and the sea of memories parted to create a path to the door. On each side, everyone faced me and I stepped forward to walk the gauntlet of my mind, feeling the blows from all those who I felt I had in some way failed.

Kent and Willis walked me outside and down a sidewalk to their car. I turned my head to take one last look at the house and saw Chase standing in the illuminated doorway with his back to me. Everyone else I'd seen in the house was gone. He disappeared inside and I heard the slightest scratch of a needle being lifted. I'm sure the record stopped spinning, but in my mind the music grew louder.

ACKNOWLEDGMENTS

Many thanks to the crew at Down & Out Books for their continued support of my work. I cannot adequately express my appreciation for their friendship and professionalism. I have also received a tremendous amount of assistance and encouragement from the International Thriller Writers organization and my fellow contributors to the website The Thrill Begins. They get me. Which is rather scary. Additional thanks go to Vince Bomba and the staff at Galaxie Electronics in Pittsburgh, PA. Vince patiently taught me about turntables and record players (there is a difference) and his expertise is unparalleled. While I would like to say I drew upon my musical expertise while writing this book, I have none. Therefore, I called upon my brother, Brian Hensley, who taught me about recording studios, various instruments, and other aspects of the music industry. Thank you, Brian. Finally, I have a tremendously supportive family who have endured my many outings to bookstores, libraries, and conventions. Without their love and support, I'd be adrift.

J.J. HENSLEY is a former police officer and former Special Agent with the U.S. Secret Service. He graduated from Penn State University with a B.S. in Administration of Justice and has a M.S. degree in Criminal Justice Administration from Columbia Southern University. J.J.'s first novel *Resolve* was named one of the Best Books of 2013 by *Suspense Magazine* and was named a Thriller Award finalist for Best First Novel. He is a member of the International Thriller Writers.

Hensley-Books.com

BOOKS

On the following pages are a few
more great titles from the
Down & Out Books publishing family.

For a complete list of books and to
sign up for our newsletter,
go to DownAndOutBooks.com.

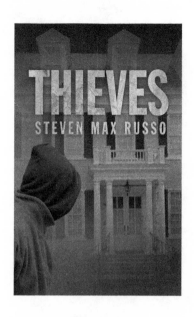

Thieves
Steven Max Russo

Down & Out Books
November 2018
978-1-948235-40-2

Dark, deadly and disturbing, *Thieves* will both horrify and delight you.

In his stunning debut thriller, Steven Max Russo teams a young cleaning girl with a psychopathic killer in a simple robbery that quickly escalates into a terrifying ordeal. Stuck in a deadly partnership, trapped by both circumstance and greed, a young girl is forced to play cat and mouse against her deadly partner in crime.

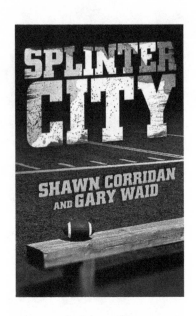

Splinter City
Shawn Corridan and Gary Waid

Down & Out Books
November 2018
978-1-948235-39-6

After nearly two decades in prison, high school gridiron great Dan Parrish returns to his hometown in rural Kansas with nothing more than a duffle bag and a desire to quietly get on with his life.

But picking up the pieces in a place where he was once revered isn't as easy as he hoped, especially for a convicted felon in the Bible Belt.

When Dan is offered a dream job—a coaching staff position with the Echo Junior College football team—he must decide between accepting the offer and risking his newfound freedom; or leaving Echo, tail between his legs, and breaking the promise he made to his dying father.

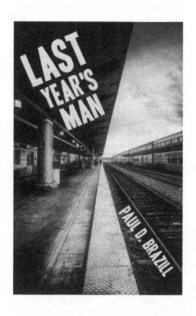

Last Year's Man
Paul D. Brazill

All Due Respect, an imprint of
Down & Out Books
978-1-946502-89-6

A troubled, ageing hit man leaves London and returns to his hometown in the north east of England hoping for peace. But the ghosts of his past return to haunt him.

Last Year's Man is a violent and blackly comic slice of Brit Grit noir.

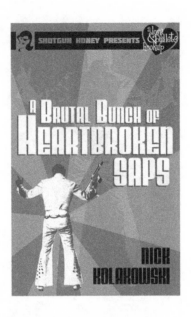

A Brutal Bunch of Heartbroken Saps
A Love & Bullets Hookup
Nick Kolakowski

Shotgun Honey, an imprint of
Down & Out Books
978-1-943402-81-6

Bill is a hustler's hustler with a taste for the high life...who suddenly grows a conscience. However, living the clean life takes a whole lot of money, and so Bill decides to steal a fortune from his employer before skipping town.

Pursued by crooked cops, dimwitted bouncers, and a wisecracking assassin, Bill will need to be a quick study in the way of the gun if he wants to survive his own getaway. Who knew that an honest attempt at redemption could rack up a body count like this?

Printed in the USA
CPSIA information can be obtained
at www.ICGtesting.com
LVHW040321220923
758957LV00020B/142